The
Second Dune

Books by Shelby Hearon

Armadillo in the Grass
The Second Dune
Hannah's House
Now and Another Time
A Prince of a Fellow
Painted Dresses
Afternoon of a Faun
Group Therapy
A Small Town
Five Hundred Scorpions
Owning Jolene
Hug Dancing
Life Estates
Footprints
Ella in Bloom

The
Second Dune

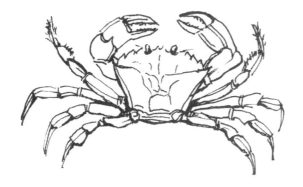

by Shelby Hearon

Afterword by James Ward Lee

TCU Press
Fort Worth, Texas

The Texas Tradition Series Number Thirty-Four
James Ward Lee, *Series Editor*

Library of Congress Cataloging-in-Publication Data

Hearon, Shelby, 1931-
  The second dune / by Shelby Hearon.
    p. cm. -- (Texas tradition series ; no. 34)
  ISBN 0-87565-273-5 (trade pbk. : alk. paper)
  1. Women--Texas--Fiction. 2. Mothers and daughters--Fiction. 3.
Remarried people--Fiction. 4. Texas--Fiction. I. Title. II. Series.

PS3558.E256 S43 2003
813'.54--dc21
                                          2002154064

Cover Design by
Barbara Mathews Whitehead

For Wendy Weil—her book

FOREWORD

In my first novel, *Armadillo in the Grass,* I wanted to write about a woman bounded by her parents, husband, children, house, as we women were at the time. But I couldn't make it work, that narrow family-bound account, until she transcended the domestic with a life's work that she loved—until she became a sculptor. But the second time around, in *The Second Dune,* I tried again to create a woman who would be valued the way we valued our grandmothers and their mothers, for who they were, not what they did.

Having grown up a geologist's daughter, I chose to use my love of the physical world—its ancient remnants of life, its upheavals, its oceans—to give my narrator a very particular view of the world. One which I hope makes her believable to the reader when she says: *Born by the sea, I think in geologic time.*

It pleases me to have Ellen and her story back in print, now that I am living between two glacier-gouged mountain ranges, on a lake once vast and deep, whose shores are rife with fossils.

Shelby Hearon
Burlington, Vermont
2002

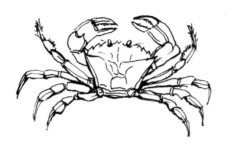

The female land crab, having returned
to the sea to spawn, repeats the long journey
inland past predatory sea birds, across the sand
dunes beneath a scorching sun, to make her home
at last by some waterhole which will moisten
her gills and quench
her thirst.

The
Second Dune

ONE

Friday, May 5

We search for signs of the sea, my daughter and I. It is our morning ritual on this dry limestone escarpment that once was an ocean floor. Picking with our fingers for fossils in the dusty buff *caliche* cliffs, we walk in May's white sun across the bottom of a great Cretaceous sea.

An unexpected wind blows, damp. I feel as if spring has grown desperate to crack this still, flat, lacquered sky, to shake loose water from its bowl. After a fall dry as rattling bones, a winter baking hot as summertime, the weather has brought us extremes, has frozen and cracked our ground, blown gales of dust, scorched back the heat, then, this week, as if exhausted, fallen quiet as an amber hush before a storm. The wind feels good; we are still parched from last year's bitter drought, a choking reminder of the dustbowls of the thirties and fifties. We cannot get enough of rain on this dry hill.

Today we find a dozen or two slow-moving, bottom-dwelling pelecypods. Looking like ordinary oyster shells from my parents' home in Galveston, they go into a cotton sack to be taken back to edge a bed of blue plumbago beneath a live oak in the garden.

We like to scatter life as old as dinosaurs and as hard as rock among the blooming flowers of my yard.

Ellen Nor, sturdy, dragging her stuffed elephant with her, finds a gastropod as big as her fist. Triumphant with its size, she digs it out, scrapes it from the crumbling creamy clay of the hillside.

She hunts with me in vain for the flattened rounds of echinoids, cousins of the sand dollar, who once lived in clusters in the shallows here. These are the chief goals of our long hot walk today. Ellen Nor enjoys the search. Looking along the path, she calls them by familiar names that sound like treats from our kitchen: biscuit urchins, sea cucumbers, sea strawberries. We do not find these foods of the sea; it is rare to come upon them intact, their backbones are too fragile.

Born by the sea, I think in geologic time.

Einstein made public what was clearer than daylight on our hill: time is not a constant thing. It all depends on where you stand and whether you are moving toward it or away, a relative thing. It depends on whether you are pacing the dragging hours out waiting for a courtroom and divorce, or climbing a flight of stairs to hasten through the speeding hours of a love still clandestine.

The clock-world of my grade school made time less clear, not more. It jumped by bells for us; it froze for those in our readers: they never let Dick get wrinkles or Jane have menopause. Spot and Puff never grew lame and blind. As a small child I had lived in the time of fairy tales, where the seventh son of the seventh son combs the seven seas for seven scales, while the princess remains unaltered, nubile, waiting: a castled Penelope, east of the sun and west of the moon. During the same years, on Sundays, the Bible was full of lessons on the implacability of fourscore and ten: Job got older and fell on bad times; Ruth sheaved her way to another husband and some acreage.

None of these ways to measure duration provides for the fact that time runs both ways at once, like the ocean's tide going out and coming in. Here as we stand on early Mesozoic, who is to say that seventy million years ago is not the present too. Farther north of us, up a river, a shove of granite reveals the bottom of the Paleozoic; yet that outcropping from the ages past is no less visible now than my daughter, who is four, as humankind keeps track of itself.

Ellen Nor sits down to rest, to watch the river flow below. When she sits in the heat like this, sweat rolls down the underside of her legs, making it wet behind her knees. She sweats a mustache on her upper lip.

The essence of the love we mothers have for daughters is distilled in what we convey to them of all that we have learned about being female. In what time we have we must sort out the truth as we have lived it, and hand it on. Out of this grail-passing love, an intense and not always helpful affection, I speak silently to some man in my daughter's future, aware that even in her day men will attempt to define her: "Don't love this girl for reasons which obscure her meaning; don't love her for her shape or smile. Love her because she sweats a mustache and drips behind her knees. Love her because her hands are fierce and digging."

Raised by women, schooled by women, we who are mothers now were taught to look across the gulf to men and count ourselves only as they counted us. We learned to take our hearts and wrap them in ribboned boxes to be raffled at socials to the dark one on the right.

As schoolgirls, we had daytimes of boys; in bed at night we had only our pillows to lay against our burning cheeks. Marriage changed that sequence; the score was kept on different cards. Their attachment to us safely legalized, men departed our day, to return to us only in the evening when their work was done.

Although we thus learned early to tune our ears to the language of men, it is from female to female that the Word is passed. It is my mother's control—when storm winds have racked her garden, lashed years of her work into a pile of fallen leaves and branches, left her standing on the back porch surveying a hurricane's cruel devastation and saying only, "The storm took an important tree," then going in the house to get her garden gloves to start again—that formed her daughter Ellen. As it is her mother—hand-stitching a galaxy of green-tipped stars upon a sea of quilts until her eyes made water and her thimbles wore smooth—that formed her. It is this backbone of the species that makes my daughter confident.

As she is now, as she gets up and says, "We need to go eat, Mama." Assuming I will follow.

Which I do, behind her and the tired stuffed elephant who bumps along the path. The wind dies down as we go back home on the long winding unpaved road that circles the hill above our house—a new hill as hills are measured, recently uplifted, still visibly layered, untortured by the earth's deep heat; an old house as houses are judged, made of blocks of the same massive limestone that forms the hill. We live with John in this house set into and made of its surroundings (not like my mother's Victorian island set with its gingerbread back to the sea), in an early Texas two-story with wooden beams, and porches top and bottom. A deep, cool house. And mine.

Coming in from the outside I move automatically among the house plants as if they shared our thirst, poke into the soil to feel the depths of dryness, water the white begonias, pinch a dead leaf off the potted agapanthus lilies that bloom, on necks as willowed as the great blue heron's, by the sunporch window.

We have our luncheon, laid out as my mother taught me, on linen mats, with flowers in a bowl and silver spoons for our soup. We girls deserve it so. As is our custom, we save back sandwich scraps for later to feed the dogs who live with their masters to the east of us.

These dogs, called Bruno and Siegfried by their owners, called, more properly, Fang and Wolf by us, tend to run disorderly through my life. Too frequently they leap the rock wall into my garden, pawing at the blooms, appearing in the wrong time of day. I prefer to invite them over in the later afternoon, in the time of day given to interruptions. It is my way to try, by offering them thawing chicken gizzards or a bite of cold lunch ham, to limit their appearance to a scheduled time of day.

Ellen Nor buffers me against the dogs by her casual lack of fear. She likes to take my hand and lead me past their jaws, looking after me, her mother. She is at ease in her female role of looking-after; is equally at ease in our world of girls and in the outside world. In this she is like a mid-tide limpet, that rarity at home both in the sea, its keyhole safely covered in the primacy of water, and on the land, its mantle bared to scavengers. Soft as any mollusk, tenacious more than most, it clings by a foot to the rocks and rides out every tide. With the same style, Ellen Nor goes undismayed from our world of fossil hunting and orderly lunches to the outside yard with its dogs or the downtown streets with their traffic.

We go upstairs to settle her for her nap. I make promises that allow her to give up the waking state. "We will feed the dogs when you wake up."

"Bad dogs," she says happily. "Good Bombay."

I wipe her stuffed pet off and fix his wobbly eye. His name hurts my ears, and his too, from the looks of him. He looks as if flies bite his back in a mudhole too, far from the sound of the Indian Ocean. He remembers better times; elephants remember.

He was named by John—my new husband, as husband's go, Ellen Nor's old daddy, as her life goes—who made a great adventure out of finding his origin and a great story out of naming birthday presents. He carried my daughter and her beast into the library to consult the globe and all the reference books, taking up space as if he were himself the largest animal on land. After checking all the sources he pronounced the new arrival Asian and not African, and flopped its ears for his daughter to see. Lifting up her hair he found and kissed her ears. A bedtime play of ears before he carried them both upstairs, with her dark hair on one shoulder, and the elephant resting his identifying lobes on the other.

The pet came from the elaborate gift floor of our

best department store, a floor displaying imported crystal, carved compotes, topiary trees, Chinese vases large enough for Ali Baba. He was standing in a grouping with a brass game table and an ivory chess set. She found him after she had walked impassive through two floors of clothes and one of toys and not been at all impressed with what was being offered girls turned four.

She spotted him from the escalator and threaded her way carefully to him, not bumping expensive things, or alerting saleswomen. "I'll take him," she said to me, reaching down and lifting him out of his decorative context into a more correct milieu. Holding him, she completed his jungle look. Her coloring an echo of his mahogany color, she looked a miniature Rousseau face, peering through the foliage of a plastic rubber tree.

It was the same certainty she had shown when she chose a brand new name. She was my namesake, a smaller Ellen. But when she was three and all her cakes were decorated with a trinity, serene that it was her due, she asked me for another, longer name. One that was not to be shared. So we picked Eleanor, which decorates itself on her as Ellen Nor: two bigger proper names. It doesn't always stick: John calls her his Baby Ellen; my brother Edward, attached to the diminutive, calls her Ellie. But she and I never say it wrong.

I make her one last promise. "Frank will wake you." She smiles to think of that, loving this big brother who has another father.

"I'll pull down the blinds to make some shade. Pretend you are under the big oak tree."

Tucked in, she lids her eyes as I close the door and go downstairs to wait for Frank, coming home from school.

Afternoons belong to children and their friends, to neighbors and their dogs.

Such orderly rules make up my days, as unvarying as the processes that wear mountains down to sand. Like heat, cold, wind, and water, outside, inside, children, solitude, and John take their turns through my mornings, afternoons, and evenings. It is this routine that turns my days on the axis of my woman's mid-tide life.

My son and I don't get on too well, he being twelve. At the sound of his car pool door, I put on a record, a rock piece he likes that I like also. It sounds to me, underneath its beat, like the straining pipes of a church organ. I hear it as medieval music; although loud and electric, it remains a cry for grace. I want to please him —this tall, young son of mine. He stays removed from me, distant, treats me as a woman who cheated behind his father's back. He seems to be still struggling to understand how a grown woman could want so much to do what I did with this man who has lived with us for

five years now. The selfishness is what rankles: mothers
are not made for joy.

"What a fake thing to do," Frank says, coming in
the door. He turns off the record.

"I like the piece." Mother is put on the defensive.

"If you like it so much you have seven hours to play
it while I'm gone. That's twenty-eight times. At least
twenty-eight times. It's really fake to put it on when
you hear the car door slam."

He is precisely right. "Mothers are apt to be fake,"
I concede, prone to truth.

"You've had a lot of practice." He throws this line
over his bony shoulder, not having quite enough nerve
to say it to my face. He gauges correctly how far he
can go without being sent to his room.

I let it go. "What are you doing this afternoon?"

"Messing around. DeWitt and Brewster are coming
over."

"There are some cookies." I fall victim to the
mother's role.

He indicates indifference. "If we get hungry."

"I promised Ellen Nor you would wake her."

"That baby. What does she still have to go to sleep
for when she goes to bed the minute supper's over?
That baby." He could be my brother Edward so skill-
ful is his disdain.

I want to reach up and push the hair out of his eyes,
to tell him to stand up straighter because he is so thin

his chest looks as if it is caving in. I move in his direction, but stop a safe three feet from him.

He is ill at ease, looks around.

My tone becomes the firm voice mothers use. "You can wake her in a little while."

He hears his peers on the back porch, decides it is not time to be caught in this encounter and relents. "Sure," he says, "Okay, Mom, after a while." He exits awkwardly, stage left, toward the kitchen to intercept the boys and find the cookies.

The essence of the love one has for sons is that we must stand them on their feet and let them go, to group themselves with other men, to group themselves by peers. Constrained by culture and our own past experience from intimacy with them, we disengage them at an early age. From this strong cord-cutting love reserved for sons, silently I wish the retreating back of this boy the best I have to offer him: "Don't break your neck with your own hands."

Edward taught me how to deal with Frank. One scene of many with my brother comes to mind: I am showing him my wedding dress. I am caught in the magic of that moment when, dressed all in symbolic white, you become someone else—the imagined you, a fairy tale princess, a legend, a vestal virgin, a bride. You know the image in the mirror is not reality, but it doesn't matter. What does matter is that you have created it from your childhood's dreams to offer to a waiting groom. In my case, Franklin. Edward breaks the spell, saying in an offhand tone, "Not bad, Rima. For a Bird Girl. But do something with the front; makes you look flat as two strawberries on an ironing board."

My brother taught me how to maintain the slender contact that boys permit females who are not for sex. You have to learn that to love them well is to show it little, that insult is their safeguard to keep you at your distance, as they require a space between you. Above all you have to learn to deal with them through other males.

This operates in my house now: I am allowed to bring coffee to Edward when he comes to visit and talks legal medicine with John, or to listen in as Frank tells his stepfather enviously about Grayson's brother's car with Koni shocks and Holley carbs.

One special relationship that one must leave alone is that of a son with his father. And that is the very one that I restricted when I took Frank from Franklin. As Frank grows to look increasingly like his father—a slender man, neatly put together—my guilt grows also, confronted with a visible daily reminder.

In the kitchen I find cookie crumbs and footprints. I plug in the pot of afternoon coffee. There is no point in going back over the decision to leave Franklin; it was difficult enough at the time.

Even after I was meeting John, even after I had persuaded myself that everyone would be better off, it took so long to break the news to Franklin. What held me was the strength of our routine, the pull of his unvarying consistency. We had our days so ordered that there was no scheduled time to admit my unfaithfulness, to mention that which was outside the pattern of our time inside the cooling walls of home.

Breakfast continued as it always had: a slice of wholewheat toast, an egg, a grapefruit halved and sectioned with a paring knife. We had our pot of morning coffee while Franklin read aloud the headlines: the public was displeased with LBJ. There was no moment between the grapefruit and the egg to interpose my going, as there was none, by candlelight for two, between the clear tomato soup and the lemoned fish toasted on the edges from the broiler.

In the mornings in a rented room—my garden then a papered wall finer than a bed of Talisman roses—I asked John what to do. "Listen, love, how can I tell him?"

Finally, I intruded in the only place such news seemed possible. I went to Franklin's office at the bank. There, in a surrounding arranged for trustees of estates, a business setting, we made an interval to discuss divorce.

"At least then you'll have to get along without me.

Fathers who are divorced have to speak to their sons directly."

"It is you who has trouble speaking plainly; I was not receiving the message that we were not doing fine."

"I was sending it but you were too busy gluing tiles at your mother's farm."

"Frank is too young to be uprooted, Ellen."

"He needs to live with a man who doesn't need a go-between. Who won't turn me into my mother."

"Are you telling me there is someone else?"

It was a hard blow to deal to a slender clock-run man who never seemed to age, the kind of man who only stoops as the years go by, bending more and more into himself until he dies, cocooned.

It was unfair to take him from this boy whom he now sees on alternate weekends, as our custody schedule continues as unvarying as our life before.

Children home, mothers come together like birds at a feeder. Karol, my neighbor on the west, comes over. We take cups out onto the glassed sunporch to enjoy the green of the rarely rained-on yard through air-conditioned space. Karol and I are old friends; husbands ago we were friends. She has hair too black, stretch pants too tight. She wears the giveaway air of looking for a man. She runs a small travel agency to support herself, her girls and a bedridden mother given to nagging her to get married again, as does the world. Left alone, Karol does all right.

We talk about our schools—black and white and scared all over in their new desegregation. Which is a long way from integration.

She bites a fingernail, and says, "Looks like we made it today, without a riot. I've been jumpy as bare feet on asphalt. I kept the girls home yesterday; Black Nancy kept her girls home, too. You try not to panic, but all those rumors going around . . ."

"Frank said it was going okay." Reluctantly obliging when he was asked by his mother for some comment on his outer world.

"How can you stay so out of it? I think about it all the time. They scare me; I can't help it. They look right through you like you weren't there, those kids."

They. She does not see that all of us living on this inclined uplift are *we. They* are pelecypods gathered by the handful on the beach, their gentle hook protruding above a ridged and curving flange. *They* are in my jar of shells. Another millennium and *we* will calcify to *they,* our bones picked from the solid sediment by mutated fingers under an older sun.

I try to tell Karol I cannot tell the difference: that at parents' night we were as alike as sand dollars, the same design on all our fragile faces. "When I went to

P.T.A.," I say, "all the mothers had been to the beauty shop, and all the fathers said, 'It can't be my boy; I've taught him to mind, whipped him with my belt!' "

Karol says, "They confiscated seven belts in last week's riot."

"I met their daddies."

She is not easy with it. "But the rumors. That they strangled seven white dogs. That they're going to kill two girls in every school."

"White dogs?" Ritual sacrifice?

"White people's dogs. It was just a rumor. Nancy heard black dogs." She hunts for the silver lining—needing optimism. "It will be better next year. Bound to be. The first year of anything is always the worst."

It takes more than a little while to turn a species gray, to round it at the edges. "You expect too much," I say, "Too much, in too little time."

"I know you don't miss him," she says, twisting in her chair, patting her pockets out of long habit for the cigarettes she no longer smokes, "but I do. I miss Franklin Hawkins when things get like this."

It is her style to call us by our complete names. At first I thought this was to disown her kin; now I think it is a way of giving them a distinction apart from possession. She never says *my daughter* or *your husband*. She calls her own girls Molly Surrey and Sally Surrey. Even our shared help she never calls *my maid*, but always Black Nancy. And properly so; in Texas Nancy's given name is "Black."

"If Sally Surrey," she tells me, "got raped tomorrow by one of them in his big afro, Franklin would come over and frown that frown," she demonstrates, "and say, 'We have some recourse here, I'm sure.' "

She does him well. Recourse was his word. It was his style as well. I tell her, "You can come to John instead. Everyone does. And he can sue."

"Oh, John. He'd have to settle back in that big chair with his shoes off like he does, like a candidate in a candid shot, and ruminate about his family. Can't you just hear him? 'Why, Karol, that's just like the time old Billy Bob knocked up my sister. Why we nearly had to run him out of town. You know my sister was the prettiest gal that ever twirled in the Cotton Bowl parade!' " She is cheering herself up with her mimicry.

She does John well, too: everything that happens has happened before to John. Having a precedent, he is comfortable with all events. I make a small correction: "He has no sisters."

Anxious, now that we talk of men, Karol repairs a bitten fingernail.

I ask, "How did it go with Pete?"

She rolls her eyes around, indicating impossible. "Next time you and John Marshall matchmake me with a widowed doctor friend, don't get somebody with hay fever. After watching him blow his W. C.

Field's nose all through dinner, I wasn't getting into bed. What would he do with his handkerchief?"

"John says Pete is allergic to germs. That cancer gives him hives. Not a bad thing for a doctor." John has a tale for every friend; a lot of tales.

Karol has other news. "Would you believe a warehouse salesman named Nookie? I mean he sells warehouses?"

Nookie? "Not very well."

"Sometimes I do suspend good judgment."

"Where did you find him?"

"Another gift of mutual friends like you." She wears a hopeful look, bites again the fingernail.

We talk about our families. Women do that, take on one another's kin. It is the bond: I'll worry for yours, if you'll worry for mine. An entire family is too much soap opera for one woman alone.

We cover her ailing mother; we discuss her daughters, who are wild and soon to be in trouble. She asks after my brother's pregnant wife.

"She is still carrying it. Or not yet miscarrying it. But she isn't doing well."

"What will they call it when it comes? You have such a dynasty. Eddie for your dad, or Edward for your brother? Won't this be the third? Maybe they can call him Ned, that's British. Or Ted, that's presidential."

"When Laura Ann does carry one it will probably be Edwina."

"Pity her. I think I left Bob Surrey for the look on his face when they told him his second was another girl."

I laugh at that. "Sally was ten when you left—"

"It grew on me. I don't move fast. One morning I woke up and looked at him asleep beside me, holding on to himself with one hand and the pillow with the other, and I thought: you inseminating egotist. And called my mother."

"Your mistake."

"At least she doesn't snore." She looks away from that bad time, out to the leafy green of May across the yard.

We watch the afternoon birds picking supper from the sprinkled grass.

She says, "It looks like a florist shop, but I would hate to see your water bill. I can't afford around-the-clock hoses. If we don't get some rain by July mine will be the Gobi desert." She looks around. "Where is the heir?"

"He's messing around."

"Aren't you glad at least he isn't into girls. Who is it today? He's never by himself."

"DeWitt and Brewster."

"What happened to boys named Butch and Stud?"

21

"They had DeWitt and Brewster. And the other one is Grayson."

"Everyone is named for his grandfather's county obviously. Even Franklin, Jr."

It is true. Thin, familied Franklin.

"I guess Nookie is a little-known county in Texas. Out there by Deaf Smith." She jollies herself.

The sun comes out, steaming us here on our layered hill. Heat waves rise off the grass like early mists from hot new seas. The birds step into the shade.

"Time to get back. My siesta is over. Back to help the crappy people who fly to Mexico for Fun and Enchantment. See the world on Bank Americard." She opens the screen door.

I wait for her postscript, which is sure to come.

She sticks her head back in; all her worries are done as afterthoughts. "At the health spa last night rolling my behind I saw this woman go into the sauna with scars that took off half her shoulder. I felt for lumps all night and had to take two sleeping pills to get to sleep."

My room is my oasis. My waterhole. A wildebeest I, trudging up the stairs alone. My mother still speaks of this as her mother's Green Room, as if she were descended from the White House where the rooms have names, so positive was my grandmother's intrusion into her daughter's life. For my grandmother who grew up in this old stone house this was a space to quilt in the clear light of the north, quilting stars of patchwork apple green. For me, now, it is a seascape: a room washed in palest celery, a canvas of waterlilies by Monet. It is the green of the underside of leaves, grass lightened with dew, the sea on a rainy day. The pale carpet, the cotton coverlet bound in silk, the chaise, sheer curtains layered like thicknesses of spiderweb to mute the light, all aim at the translucence of a certain depth of water.

Preparing myself for John, as carefully as if we were still meeting, unlawful, in the mornings, instead of wedded and encumbered in the husband time of day, I wash myself. Showering under chlorinated rain, under simulated odorless rain, I open all my hair. So much of me is dependent on this heaviness of hair, its weight, its presence; it is a mantle I go under like Rapunzel, or a bare Godiva.

Or mermaid. Come out of the sea to man.

But I have not come out to stay, only to visit. Like the waterfowl, with regularity I migrate back.

Each year on the second of June I make an annual trip alone to watch the world break whole, climbing a new day over the edge of the sea, making me a year older. This pilgrimage to home, to all my earlier selves, has not varied through two husbands. It is a birthday present to myself: myself. It is a return to the beach that is the backdrop for all the scenes I play.

There, earlier Ellens still lie, like surfaced fossils, for the gathering. There, in the dimensions of that shore, all the Ellens live: only the time of their existence shifts.

In the daytime, Galveston beach is the tattered public beach of other people's words. My mother says she hasn't been down in ten years, that no one goes. Meaning no one she knows. Daddy says it is no fun when you can't tell the boys from the girls. Young mothers find it hazardous: cars, riding almost to where the sand is wet, make speed in both directions; riderless surfboards crash onto the shore like loose planks in a hurricane. Frantic fish, almost on the surface of the water, appear to rise from the surf for air. The Gulf of Mexico is now a turbid wash, its bottom gone from sight, the beach a litter of beer-clotted garbage and bounding dogs. For collectors there are only the shards of shells in the daytime.

But it is not this beach I home to, whose bellied crowds come to be carmelized by the sun, renting umbrellas, oiling themselves, hanging out veined breasts and heavy pones, turning red and blistering.

I go in the shadows to the water, in the early morning's half light, when there are only a few campers' tents, a few blanketed lovers, the cleanup crew bouncing in their dunebuggies.

Staying at my mother's I get up before someone else's sunset becomes our dawn, to see the Gulf still

gray around the edges, piers casting shadows gray as
salt-bleached boards. To watch on the horizon masted
ships slipping in like a line of oryxes, dispersing in the
light.

It is the deserted time when seagulls feed; alongside
sandpipers and crested terns they stand in formation on
the sand, patterning themselves like geese in flight,
picking their black feet carefully at the lapping edge,
making breakfast. The sun, returning from the east,
rises at an angle showing the upward curve of Texas'
coast, a glowing ball floating out of the water. East
light at your left when eating from the sea; sunburn on
your right flank when opening a beer in the afternoon.

Galveston's ancient sand barrier island, formed during a standstill in an ancient sea, backs against a bay
once shallow enough for cattle to cross, before money
made digging out the living oysters an industry.

At one time glaciers ground mountains of ice against
an earlier shore, at one time a river's mouth was buried
by the melt; the geometry of these changes has left
coastwide terraces and lagoonal shallows. Evidence of
these changes suggests also a feeling of shifting sand beneath our feet, of tomorrow not being like today, of
our own shore changing or disappearing with the night.
The living sea makes time more visible than the rigid
faulted cliffs at home where prior existence is set as
hard as stone.

At dawn six years ago I went down with the whitened gulls, wandering barefoot for miles (or hours, whichever is the longer), walking toward the climbing sun as it rose from daybreak's yellow to noon's incandescent white. Taking too long for everyone, I vacillated like the shoreline over a decision already made. We humans have not found a seagull's way to leave the morning when the morning leaves us. We stay to reason till the heat becomes too great and the waves too high.

My coming down to the beach at night distresses my mother; it is not proper for a woman. She fears my being mugged, as before my marriages she feared my being raped . . . But the sand is a private world when the ocean breaks under sun-reflected light, as the moon, offering its seas as a mirror, shines a path on the world's water cover. Then, bivalves as coarse and thick as gravel burrow into the sand, out of reach of grasping blue crabs. Then, the ebbing water drawn by the fingers of the moon uncovers the tide's strip, and snails slip from sight, only to pull themselves out again by the transparent protruding lip of their existence under cover of the returning film of water that stops just short of the wave before, an echo only, as the tide goes predictably out.

There are as many inhabitants as in New York City visible beneath my feet, mollusks rooting for their life pumping food-laden water through their gills, sifting their supper from the dappled waves. Humans have not learned to move their toes from crabs as fast as these bivalves in the down-straining earth-tugging receding fringe of dark water.

Quieter than such a moonlit night is the joining of wave and sand under a black and starless sky, when darkness you can see through like black glass is lit only by the crash of breakers shattering into whiteness.

Such a black allows a bathing suit to be slipped off, useless as a locust's skin. It allows my bare and rounded body to plunge into the thrust of water spilling against the earth. Swimming out into the tide until the shoreline disappears, holding the suit in one hand and rowing with the other, I can move as unseen as any other ocean dweller, carried by the current downshore—far above the deep scattering layer below which dwell the uncountable bulk of life on our planet, who travel the bottom, eating one another. Phosphorescence breaks into bits of luminous crystal on the whitecaps as I, in my suit again, swim back to shore.

There at that water's edge are many Ellens.

Ellen, small, suited for the beach. Not as safe as in mother's house or garden, needing a hand to hold to, but finding it a shock to stand against the bare hairy legs of a father out of his trousers. There is the impact of the first wave against her back, which knocks away her feet, and leaves a mouth of salt and the weight of hanging onto life by a father's hand. As fear becomes elation, Ellen's head, a cap of white, bobs with the waves until, in exhaustion, she stretches out, spent as a running dog, on the sand to sleep beside her pregnant mother.

Twelve years later the taste of salt still remains, but added to it now is the smell of baby oil and iodine—the magic mixture for a copper skin. Ellen is a Gauguin native now, black hair roping to the waist, flowers worn behind the ear—hibiscus bloom or crape myrtle, cape jasmine with its sugared smell, or, at the least, a bitter sprig of oleander, white.

Walking all the way to the beach from home, down the old walks, the brick streets, the boardwalk, she is as proud as a peddler with a basket on her head. She looks, my mother said, as dark as any Mexican and no better than one, going out like that with everything showing in broad daylight.

She goes out with everything showing but not yet touched; her halter not yet untied at the neck to reveal her breasts, her briefs not yet untied at the hips and pulled down in the sand. She, still a package just for looking, wearing stain and oil, revolves her hips in a slow and practiced strut and spreads out a towel to sun on with a shark design in red and gold. She departs that beach for college as chaste as when she swam at four by her father's legs. She leaves behind a vivid

longing to be uncovered, untied, which remains unful-
filled in the baking salty morning of sixteen.

Six years later, center of gravity off balance on the
land, knees awkward at locking and bending, spine
curving too much under its load, breasts and belly
dragged by gravity, Ellen returns to a wet supporting
world that buoys up the back, washes against her baby
like a continual caress, takes her loose ropes of hair and
floats them like seaweed on the crest of every wave.
She slips tirelessly under the breakers with a dolphin's
inborn ease.

Lying on her back like a pear-shaped seal, she pad-
dles with her toes and strokes beneath her belly Franklin's child . . . The water washes over, blurring, and
it is John's child now. Ellen, still in sea suspended, as
in an amniotic fluid, floats in weightless comfort.

Once back on land, a mermaid out, she feels the baby
settle and her back aches; her feet are sharply reminded
that it is a husband's dry-land world.

I remember reading a paper on the beginning of life
when I was lying in joy with John and thinking of
beginning Ellen Nor, a new life of my own. In it, L. V.
Berkner set out the theory that existence on our planet
took its first breaths in warm volcanic springs, shallow
as a rain pool, transient as a flash flood's leaving, caught
for the instant of creation between a new green earth
and an early early ocean. He said life waited, a mutant

stored and at the ready, for a shift in atmosphere to make it possible. It seemed to me that we began as an amino acid searching for a warm lagoon to nest in. That we were from the start searching for a place to catch our breath.

We catch it now by the shallow tidal pool of the Gulf that sways fresh and salt by turns along an undulating coastline whose newly sifted sand was silted on the back of older shores. We catch it now by an afternoon sea.

However much we may believe in the days and nights of rain that created our creators, however much the collective subconscious remembers the painful crawl of our lung-breathing ancestors from the great Cretaceous waters, however atavistically woman may long for the sleeking rounding Pliocene oceans, those seas of our world's mornings are now uplifted, shifted, compacted, and transformed, a glove turning itself inside out, a mountain falling into the earth, an unsteadiness rising into a mountain, water evaporating into the millenniums of condensation.

Our morning sea is now that arid cleft *caliche* on the hill. Our afternoon sea is the tide that daily wets our feet, that feeds us in our allotted span.

Wrapped in a quilted garden-flowered robe, I brush my hair with a brush made of tortoise shell as dark and polished as the wide-plank floor beneath the rug. I tend the ferns, placing Ellen Nor's gastropod like a giant snail between two ruffled leaves.

The room is as silent as a primeval fern forest before the first footsteps fell. Its curtains drawn against the heat, it is aloof from the speeding world below. Order lies upon it everywhere, as glistening as dew. And as essential.

Below I hear his voice. "Hey, Baby Ellen, you've got a kiss for Daddy?"

John creates sound, as John collects people. When he comes up the walk there are dogs, bike horns, voices where before there was only concrete and heat. Inside the house there is a gathering. He must miss his own family, in the Big House, as they call the home where they lived when their parents were living, he and his four brothers who, as boys, lined up to slide down the banisters and throw themselves at Papa. Now John, grown himself into a Papa, has only a slender pair to greet him.

The husband coming home for dinner is a cultural volume. If it is not the turning of your body toward him, the waking of your ears to the sound of him and your eyes to the sight of him, then at the least it is the lifting of the load for which you took the job. *It is never nothing.* I have had it both ways. Have heard the voice of Franklin and thought, oh, you, and, straightening up my vertebrae, come down to check the soup, receive a kiss, share a drink. Now, in a leap of faith overcoming the uncertainty of our response, the faithlessness of our bodies, the fickleness of our hearts, I hear John's voice and think, *ah, you.*

Without the coming-home the work of growing the young is a matter tended to in a school of years. Without the coming-home there is a family but no marriage. A cart without a horse. In a spell of waiting, I've had that, too.

"How's old Bombay? Looks like the eye is drooping?"

"He's still taking his nap, Daddy. On that side."

I turn the brush and press it to my face—brushing is better done with his hands when it becomes a hundred strokes and we have time alone—as I await his footsteps on the stairs.

"Frank, you boys were having some bicycle race rounding that corner. Don't you ever look out for cars? Ten speeds aren't going to help you when you get hit by a Mack truck."

"Grayson got this new Mercier and we went over to try it out." Frank never quite says, "John," and yet he can't say, "Dad." Always at the end of his sentences, polite and full of news, there is a pause in which he doesn't call a name.

At least the dialogue is pleasant now and full of the common ground of bikes and cars. Better than at the start of our living with John, when seven-year-old Frank answered his stepfather only when he had to, and never looked directly at him. That first year he came between us whenever possible; he liked to ride his training bike back and forth across the brick floors of the house when we were trying to talk.

He brought up old allegiances, making of John's presence one long comparison; "My Daddy used to," or, "My Daddy does it this way," or, with Friday just a day away, "I need to tell my Daddy tomorrow." And if he—now that the plate of cookies on the counter is his, and the *derailleur* gears in the garage are his wheels —treats John as a guest in his own house, well, he is at least a welcome guest.

"Hey, come in here with me, you two. Where's your mother? I've got a surprise for her. Open the door and look who came home with me."

Ellen Nor lets out the secret. "Frank, Frank, do you

know who's here? It's Uncle Ed without his Laura."
My daughter keeps track of missing girls.

"Gee, Uncle Ed, that's great. Do you want to see my
new bike?" Frank is not at a loss for words around his
hero.

From below I hear the entrance of my brother, turning me into a sister.

Edward spends his life popping up unannounced. As
if he were still hiding in the back seat of my date's car,
jumping up, roaring with laughter, when the boy
turned off the ignition and leaned across to me.

He never gives me notice that he is coming, knowing
that would give me time to refresh my memory of our
kinship, time to gather myself from waiting for John
to assume a jollier role. Edward, grown, still likes to
wilt me with surprises.

"Ellen?" John calls for me up the stairs.

"Ellen." He finds me, brush in hand, waiting in the
foliage of my expectation.

He leans down to find my mouth, meets me leaning
up. Touching him, I shut out the sounds below. I lean
my weight against him, feel him there, and let him
hold me.

"Your hair's still wet," he says.

"Yes." I show him the brush.

"Leave it down; I like it." He takes off his tie and throws it on the bed. "Can you imagine Ed was going to drive down and back without coming out to see us? Med school has warped his mind, as I told him. I said you'd be hurt with me if I didn't bring him out to eat."

I look at evening out the window. "What is he doing here?"

"Job hunting. Interviewing. Isn't that fine? He couldn't do better than to clinic here."

This is large news to handle in my bathrobe. I take a little time to think about it, going all around it in my mind, like avoiding a toothache with one's tongue. I stall a minute. "Laura Ann didn't come?"

"She isn't feeling very good." He exchanges glances with me, trying in his large, open way to be delicate about the fact that my sister-in-law may be miscarrying still another baby. John is used to aunts and grandmothers handling these matters. He gets back to Edward. "He walked in the office just as I was leaving. I almost missed him." He sits down and eases into some looser shoes, leaving his town shoes like upended boats on my sea-green rug.

"He may move here?"

"Wouldn't that be fine?"

How could that be fine? What sort of schedule do you have with relatives in town? It will have to be something less than the communal visiting at John's brothers' houses, when all the kids are welcomed in their pajamas to pile on your bed and scatter breakfast crumbs, and dogs bound up to roll between you, tearing the morning papers. It should be more like the formality of my mother's day, when kin came after church for Sunday dinner (pickled garden cucumbers, hand-canned green beans, pecan pies) and sat around until three o'clock, when it had all been digested, and then went home.

Edward is sure to find a house in the flatlands, where the kitchens are all-electric and doctors who don't make house calls take up tennis. We'll have to be mobile and friendly and get together for drinks over his charcoal grill. Ellen Nor will have to be cleaned up and shushed and reminded that it isn't proper to watch the boy next door pee in his sandpile. Their neighbors will have poodles.

I will want to welcome Laura Ann, and pat her shoulders and tell her that it's all right if she isn't making babies. I'll bring her the first of my bulbs above ground: yellow daffodils, sweet grape hyacinths, and dwarf blue iris. I'll take her sweet peas and pinks in a yellow bowl, roses in a cut-glass vase. I'll take her potted ferns, and packets of seeds for her flatland yard: candytuft, calendula, larkspur, and verbena. What else is there to give that Edward won't snipe about but growing plants, reminders of our mother.

John is talking food. He is wanting me to do him proud before Edward. His mother left him certain that to love is to feed.

"Nancy left two chickens cooked." I offer chicken salad.

"How about that chicken enchilada pie? Something spicy would be good. I bet Ed misses that up there, Mexican food."

"I can do that."

He looses the button of his collar and drops his suit coat on my bed. "Ed and I'll get a drink and wait for you down there." He checks this with me.

"Tell him I'm on my way. Tell him I'm glad he's here." Lie for me.

The flowered robe is hung on its scented, padded hanger. The unused brush is returned to its lined drawer. Leaving my damp hair hanging down, I dress in black cotton pants and a black T-shirt—I look like a crow wading in the sprinkler. It seems the right costume for welcoming brothers.

Downstairs, John tells me they are having a little Beefeaters on ice. He hovers, like a dog wagging his tail, wanting us to get on.

"Hi." I shake my brother's hand.

"Rima," he cries, "the Bird Girl. With it all hanging out." He wraps my hair around his fist and pretends to drag me like a cave woman. The children love it.

"Wonder Boy," I retaliate, "how well you look out of your leotard."

Edward looks pleased with himself for intruding in the husband time of day. He wears the same smile he used to when, after careful calculation of the time elapsed after Daddy put his hand on Mother's shoulder and led her up the stairs, he would pretend to wake up with nightmares, beating on his parents' well-locked door.

I try to make a life he can't undo, but the effort is akin to swimming upstream.

"You're moving here?" I ask, trying not to make it an accusation.

Edward isn't fooled. "It will be all right," he says. "We won't eat your blueberry muffins."

"Do you promise?"

Edward knows his comment about the muffins will go over John's head. He made it to keep me on my toes. It is an old trick of his: he used to pretend he was going to tell my parents on me when he knew that I had done something that little girls should not do.

The muffins: when Franklin lived in my stone house we had a small celebration on Sunday mornings, a ceremony of blueberry muffins instead of wholewheat toast. We liked fresh blueberries when I could find them. It is Edward's way to get a laugh from referring to another husband beneath John's nose.

John does not understand. "I never know when you two are kidding," he says.

"We seldom are." I tell the truth.

"Humorless, Sister of Humorless," Edward explains.

My brother and I, natives both—flat high cheeks, flat black hair, legs too long for chairs, a certain nose, a certain jungle coloring—like to hone each other's edge, knowing what blood kin can take. With in-laws we are less demanding: with Laura Ann I am gentle; with my son, Edward plays the idol, with Ellen Nor he acts the doting uncle, with John he takes the role of convivial youngest brother.

We are perplexing for John. Our abrasion discomfits him, accustomed as he is to a round shoulder-slap of brothers. If there had been sisters, there would have been a kaffeeklatsch of sisters. Our person-to-person picking is too sharp for him. John likes the world to get on with itself.

He tries to show us how. Being nice, he says, "That would really be fine having you here, Ed. I know Karl and Max have a great time being in the same town." He uses his beloved younger brothers as good examples.

"It may work out," Edward says. Relaxing into an avuncular role, he lifts a four-year-old girl on his lap. "I say, Ellie, that's a pretty sad-looking animal there."

"Bombay gets a lot of wear and tear from Baby Ellen. We'll have to fix that eye."

Ellie. Baby. They decorate my daughter with these names while her half brother looks as though he could throw up. They dress "girl" with names like icing a loaf of bread to make it do for cake. This bothers me; I want this female to go by her proper name. But Ellen Nor is used to this and doesn't take it amiss.

She asks my brother, wanting an accounting, "Why did you come without your Laura?"

"She's sick in bed. But she'll be all right." He pats his niece as he would his wife.

There is a pause.

I decide we need a chance to talk of Laura Ann, as adults. It seems a fine time to take the leftover lunch outside to feed the neighbors' dogs. Taking advantage of his uncle's presence, I ask my son if he would oblige and take his sister along.

The look he gives me is not as fierce as it could be. He wants the visitor to think well of him. He tries to imitate my brother as he slouches out. In vain: he's made too neatly. Heredity will out, and Son of Franklin exits to the yard.

"Laurie's not so good," Edward answers my question. "She's spotting."

"Spotting?" I try to get some facts.

"Showing. Bleeding." He is impatient with me.

"Edward, is she miscarrying again?" I also am impatient, with his doctor's runaround.

"It looks like it."

"Why does she have to do this, Edward? Were you frightened by a fertility rite? Still sleep on the rice thrown at your wedding? Let her be. What does it do for you, the annual knock-up?"

"She says she wants a baby more than anything."

"For you."

"I'm almost thirty," he grows defensive.

"So adopt one off a reservation."

At my tone John intercedes. "I was a good bit older than that, Ed. The last one on my block. My brothers were laying bets." He leans back into a story. "You can't figure these things. In school, when I was Student Body President, I assumed I'd marry the biggest pair on campus, have six boys, and run for Governor before I was forty." He smiles, tolerant of his early self.

"You bombed out all around." Edward gazes at my chest.

"No, after a while you figure it out. That anyone can have more of it than the next fellow if he's willing to peddle for it."

"So you settled for less." Edward gestures to his sister.

"So you wait to get what no one else has."

Or, if he means me, what someone else couldn't keep. Or, if he means the law, he has created a place for himself distinct from Karl and Max and Harold, the brothers. Either way, John got there by elbowing. But he meant no offense to the crowd jostling against his elbow; winners need the crowd.

He tries now to give Edward a little advice, to show him the way it is. "You didn't marry her for children. You have to look at what you've got; Laurie isn't strong. She has the kind of skin you see right through, the kind where you can see the vein beat in her temple. You might wait awhile if this one doesn't work out."

John is kind to point out Laura Ann's fragility. It is his way to give each person full benefit. The first time we talked, in the midst of a summer crowd, he told me what a fine person my husband was, so well respected at the bank. But John presses his own interest first. At that same party, arm around my waist, he let me know that having made my acquaintance he was not to be thought of as any great friend of Franklin's.

Edward is defensive now. "Your husband is on my back." He turns his anger onto me. "It's her, not me, that doesn't take the pill."

He is trying to get out of all responsibility, but even while Laura Ann was blushing from her honeymoon, Edward was telling us how they'd have their family by the time they started practice.

That weight to produce was never set on me. Franklin—well, he got his son. And John thought a girl was news, that my having a baby for him was itself a full delight.

But that is because John is made to be delighted, not because he wouldn't have welcomed a team of children. He is congenitally pleased. His mind is affected by his body's harmony: all the valves open and close agreeably, the fluids pump happily like a producing well. However much he furrows his brow, and feels the cuts of others, his built-in good nature overwhelms. It seemed to him a part of the scheme that he should sire one daughter only—after all, his mother had an uncle who did, Uncle Otto, who is still alive at ninety to tell the tale.

Wanting Edward and me to stop our discord, John takes out another story. It is long, involved, amusing, about an aunt who, after sixteen years of trying hard, finally got pregnant by eating a pound of grapes a day . . . and had a purple baby. We laugh at this invention, and it relaxes things.

Feeling we are friendly again, John says to Edward, "You've got lots of time ahead. It takes a while to start your practice. Marcus Welby's helper has been riding that motorcycle a long time."

Edward has recovered. He rallies—back on stage. "I had more than Welby's house calls in mind. I had in mind more the battlefield scenes in *Gone With the Wind*, and *Doctor Zhivago*: outstretched hands uplifted as I go by, the wounded tearing at my clothes, shouting, 'Doctor, Doctor.' "

As I said, we seldom kid.

43

John is delighted. We are all getting on again. Telling tales. He warms up another one, much like Edward's in its overreach. "I know the feeling. I felt the same way after I passed the bar exam. I went to the first three-star restaurant I could drive to and ordered a Nebuchadnezzar of Piper Heidseck and one hundred and seventy-nine glasses. On the wall sign it said a Nebuchadnezzar was a hundred and seventy-nine glasses, so I figured the glasses should be included in the price. We were going to drink it all and smash the glasses one by one." He is delighted with this folly from his early days.

"Did they throw you out?"

"After Fred and Harold and I smashed our three glasses into the marble fireplace."

The children find us laughing, the men pretending to hurl glasses at the wall.

Supper is chicken in a jalapeño and cumin sauce almost too hot to eat. Puréed avocado for a guacamole salad makes a fresh deep green. I try to do John proud, showing off my recipes.

Edward wolfs it all; he obviously thinks himself still a growing boy. "Don't know how you turned Rima into a cook," he says to John. "A magic potion. No one else managed to." Another oblique reference to an old husband as he helps himself to more.

"John does that to everyone. You should see what Mother brings out for him, Edward."

When we had been married six months, and I hadn't gone home to press my cheek to Mother's and tell her woman-to-woman how my new marriage was, John dragged me down there, feeling I was not being a proper daughter, wishing he still had a father to show me off to. He assumed we'd stay in my old girlhood bed, and visit with the folks.

I was hesitant to go, thinking of mother's deep reservations about my leaving Franklin, whom she knew to be a gentleman, for a noisy man from a big family, who had broken up my home and made jokes at his own wedding.

But she was gracious in her polite-cool way, asking, rhetorical and Southern, "Now that you're here, John, what would you like to eat?"

John, assuming that she, like his own mother, would want to do for him, answered right away, at home in kitchens, "I surely would like some homemade buttermilk biscuits, Lillie." This with nostalgia. Biscuits triggering another memory, he asked, "And I bet you make a good soft cornbread?" He used his hands to describe it. "The kind you can hold in your hand to butter but as soft as pie."

"I make one that has no flour, only cornmeal. With bacon drippings. It isn't quite a spoonbread. That might do." She smiled, pleased to remember a recipe she hadn't made since my father went on a diet twenty years before; pleased with this hungry man I had brought to her, who slipped his arm around her waist in gratitude. That was his style and it worked on all of us.

Mother outdid herself. Dessert was a floating custard, and a fresh-grated coconut cake. Daddy, dessertless so long, regarded all this with wonder, and, under the amnesty allowed with visitors present, ate three pieces.

My daddy would have made a fine fat man if he had not been inhibited by his medical restraints. Constitutionally he is fat; his soul is fat. The way some men watch girls, he, tabooed by his obstetrics practice from ogling the female, is a voyeur of sweets.

At breakfast the second day Mother made buttermilk pecan waffles with real maple syrup. John was effusive. "Haven't had pecan waffles since we all went on Harold and Velma's honeymoon with them and ordered up six orders of waffles for all of us to eat."

After dessert Ellen Nor, who ate her supper very late for her schedule, grows sleepy. Not allowing herself to be hurried, she kisses cheeks and makes goodnights.

Frank is allowed to stay down a while with the men, he being twelve.

In repayment, by the stairs, he makes me an offer. "I'll read that baby her story."

"That would be nice."

Ellen Nor is delighted. "Frank can read," she tells me.

"That may be true." I smile at my son. I mean to suggest that he has such privacy in his life that I don't expect to know everything that goes on.

He lets a chip fall from his shoulder and says, "Uncle Ed looked at my bike and rode it up the hill. Shifting and everything." He swings his arms around, demonstrating his bike, his uncle on it.

"I'm glad you got to see him."

"Yeah. If Dad hadn't been out of town at that closing, I wouldn't have been here, would I?"

There is an awkward moment in which we are both reminded of custody arrangements while Ellen Nor tugs at her brother's hand and tries to drag him up the steps.

"Quit pullin'," Frank tells her in the same voice one uses to say: Down, Spot. Then, as if reminded, perking up, he asks me, "Did he used to do that, Mom? Pull you around by your hair?"

"Edward? Yes, much worse than that." I'm glad to cheer him up by telling him that all brothers are the same.

He looks admiring, this thin boy of mine without a beard, as he takes John's daughter upstairs to bed.

. . .

John stands when I come in. "I was telling Ed you might go back with him for the weekend. Take Baby Ellen with you. He's on call and Laura can't stay there alone. Her folks can't come down, with her Dad's bad back and all." He offers his family to help, feeling that women must need other women around to deal with woman's blood. He delegates these jobs as if in memory of a room full of aunts, heating water, knowing what to do with it.

"To Edward's?" It doesn't sound like a good idea. We have already lived with each other at another, bigger house, have already shared a bath and made fun of what the other ate for breakfast. Edward doesn't want me returning to that, now that he has a Laurie there, and, what's more, I don't want to go. I'm not the kind who comforts very well; my style is too severe.

Edward, thinking perhaps the same, doubt showing on his face, says, slightly mocking to keep it light, "We'll make you welcome." Welcome is our mother's word.

Welcome sounds like a parlor, with me seated in good dress and gloves, Laura Ann in silk, pouring tea. Which was its meaning when my mother learned the word.

But I do hesitate to think of Laura Ann up there alone—looking like a cocker spaniel who can never be patted enough, chewing her fingers, smoking her ciga-

rettes, ingesting Cokes and cookies like a child who
tries in vain to get sweet enough to be loved enough.
It is too much for Edward to use her for an incubating
machine; too much for him to expect a child to make
children. It seems to me desertion for him to leave her
to come looking for a bread-and-butter job. If I don't
go back she'll be left alone again while he does his tour
of duty where he can be reached only by the steady
paging of the hospital P.A. system. I'll have to go . . .

Edward was solicitous of his wife in the beginning;
he took pains to protect her from me. Before he introduced her, he told me, "I'm not running her down. She
is really sharp. Laurie is really sharp. But she has this
thing about her grades."
"Has what thing? A bad report card?"
"Don't be like that with her, all right?"
"Like what?"
"Like *that*." He gave the leveling look that only
brothers can give when protecting their true loves from
the judging eyes of sisters.
And I haven't been "like that" with her. I have kept
myself ready to pat her soft shoulders and send her
flowers each time she stains her panties with another
heir of Edward's.
But I don't want to leave John, not alone here in the
house, not anywhere. "What about you?" I ask him,

reminding him that Frank will be at the farm with
Franklin and his mother tomorrow and Sunday.

John waits to answer; he has something on his mind.
He moves around to get help with his words. "I'll be
gone to Houston anyway," he blurts out, looking first
at me and then at Edward. "I didn't want to bother
you all with bad news—" his voice breaks. He takes a
firmer tone. "We're all meeting at Harold's tomorrow
night; Karl and Max are flying in." He puts his foot up
on the coffee table, for ballast. He gets it out at last.
"We think Harold's wife is leaving him." He looks
away, grieving for his oldest brother.

I know what this means to him: Harold is a Metho-
dist preacher who tends them all like a flock. He is the
oldest living brother, which means he carries the added
weight of a father and another brother dead. He is a
baggy man, disorganized, for whom John would give
his life in an instant. With John and Karl and Max,
three lawyers, to help, Harold should get along.

I take the problem of the weekend off John's mind.
"Of course I'll go to Dallas," I tell him. "You go on.
I'll take Ellen Nor. She can let her elephant sleep in
that crib of Laura Ann's."

We have seen before the crib that Laura Ann keeps
perpetually prepared. She has it readied for occupancy,
threaded with velvet ribbon, stenciled with Mother

Goose: Little Boy Blue, of course, blowing his horn. It is in a separate bedroom decorated with needle-pointed pillows, stitched in blues, and a jar of candied violets.

It has waited like a sarcophagus through the two, now perhaps three, miscarriages of Edward's internship and residency. When Ellen Nor throws her beast on top of the fitted infant sheet I expect to see a wax baby, eyes fixed upon the ceiling.

My going to intrude on Laura Ann is not in keeping with the customs I grew up with. At our house Mother tended her own griefs as she did her plants, with a little digging up by the roots, some pruning, or a transplant. For the others she sent over cake; but never set her foot inside their house, never spied on their distress, or used their bathroom, or scrambled eggs in their skillet, or caught them in their gown and slippers, or in their tears. She never consented to the kind of hand-holding I have agreed to do.

It may be the decent thing to go, to let John see that we can go north and south to help our families out; for me, I'd rather burrow in the sand and wait for higher tide.

"That's too bad about old Harold," Edward says. "Divorce can be a real hassle." He slips this dig at me by my worried husband.

Frank comes in to join us; he accepts a Sprite on ice, wanting to partake like the men in an after-dinner drink. I'm not sure whom he imitates as he slouches down. It must be hard to try everyone's mannerisms on for size, searching for one that fits. It makes him seem so awkward, that not only is his voice changing, but his style is also, from room to room and audience to audience. It must take men a while to get comfortable with themselves: maybe they never do until they have a profession to put on for cover.

"We have to vote before we leave." John reminds us that the Democratic primary is tomorrow.

"Dad voted absentee," Frank says. Then, not wanting to seem unfriendly, he talks about all the candidates, because they have studied them in school. "Who are you voting for, Uncle Ed?"

"The good guys." Uncle Ed gives nothing away.

"How about the good gal?" Frank makes a joke, he hopes, laughing hollowly himself. He wants to show that he knows all about our woman candidate for governor.

"I might. Since your—since John is so worked up about her. An old pol ought to know the inside story."

John shakes his head. "I don't remember campus politics as this polarizing. We spent our time, as I recall, in simple personal slander." He tells this on his campus self. "Now each group has got a label."

"My impression," Edward says, knowing nothing of it, "is that any candidate is better than the group behind him."

John, the people's man, says, "I'd call it the other way around."

"Rima, here," Edward talks in front of me, in the habit men have, as if in the presence of infants or the retarded, "must be turned on to have a woman running. They all must; it should get out the vote."

They. My brother makes me *other* when he speaks. "You girls always . . ."; "You know women, they . . ." He should care enough to use my name.

Since women change their last names with their husbands, they have to overload with self their given names. I have inhabited both Hawkins and Marshall as if I were a visitor, as I did Maitland before that—having three surnames in three decades does not help one be at home with oneself. Women, who cannot count on being called by that profession that Frank waits and fidgets to grow into, have to learn early to answer to their proper names.

Besides, it is hard enough to live with being *Ellen* at any given place and time; it is too much of Edward to expect me to handle being *they.*

. . .

"She may get out the vote," John answers, "but I doubt it. I'll be surprised if she makes the run-off."

"Didn't you do something with the Mexican vote?"

"That's what I meant about polarizing. Sure, I got beer and tamales set up for a nighttime affair, got balloons and a bucket of campaign buttons in Spanish. But locals kept grabbing the mike hollering for Chicano power. They wanted to be considered a 'viable minority.' You couldn't find the candidate for the rhetoric."

"We'll get our fill of that at the conventions. It will be just the same; they all want their interests vested."

"It sure would be great to go to a convention, wouldn't it, Uncle Ed?" Frank is making a good grade in the democratic process at school.

"*They* who?" I ask my brother.

"Don't be like that," he chides me. To Frank he says, "You might do that. Grow up to be a politician like your old man, like John."

But of course I am "like that." Dealing with my brother causes me to be "like that." It is a response to his intention to divide us into smaller parts. I dislike the way he tracks down the myriad distinctions in the species, until the similarities between us are obliterated. He enjoys diagnosing differences, separating hiatal hernia from heart attack, and diabetics from alcoholics. His internal medicine is the dismantling of the cohesion of the body; it is as if he were taking apart a clock and making observations about time based on the examination of each spring and screw.

Edward's practice of medicine will not be the same as our father's has been . . . Edward intends dissection; Daddy offers placebo. Daddy has a sugar-coated manner that goes with patting on the head, that seems to say that all women make babies and, one way or the other, all babies come out in the end, so there is nothing to worry about. Edward will succeed in suggesting that what you are doing every day to your body's functioning is itself reason for concern. They could be in two different lines of work.

Which makes me think it isn't your profession but your personality that you practice all your life: as John practices Conviviality and calls it Law, as I would have practiced Privacy and called it Paleontology. It must be that Frank studies the men looking for a personality to wear—not seeing that his own is good enough.

It is time to climb the stairs to bed.

I send Frank down the hall, letting him give a wave, and amble off, casual, saying, "See you," over his shoulder.

I tell Edward my schedule: when I'll be up, when breakfast will be served, when the polls open, when our bags will be packed. Edward lets me know he'll get up when he feels like it.

"I'll be up soon," John says, settling down for another spell of talk.

Upstairs, later, undressing, he says, "I kept thinking Ed would ask you to come, or you would offer to go."

"We wouldn't have."

"Well . . ." He finds this hard to imagine. He reinforces that it is the right thing for me to do. "Laura will be cheered to have you up there. She'll need to have someone around, now." Obliquely, he refers to her condition.

"She may be depressed to have me in the way."

"Would you rather go down to Houston with me, take the car on down to see your mother?"

"No. You need to look after Harold. And I'll be going in four weeks anyway."

"This could count as your birthday visit, as long as I'm going anyway." He offers this, wanting me to feel invited. Taking off his at-home shoes, and tossing them beside his office shoes, he sticks to his position. "I just thought Laura would need you up in Dallas."

"It's all decided. Besides, love, it wouldn't be the same to go to Galveston now. I have to be there on *the day*." It has to do with habit, with ceremony: birds don't migrate at random times.

He looks up. "You always stick to set plans. How

can you do that?" It sounds more as if he were asking "why." "I go from crisis to crisis," he says, to show that he is the more flexible.

"You go from person to person," I say, to show that he is easy to get.

He doesn't like to think this might be criticism. "Is that so bad?"

". . . it's friendly." I smile to let that be all right.

My room is different with John in it. He likes the oversized four-poster, which reminds him of his parents' bed: it has room, even if it isn't used that way, for children to pile on with their dogs and read the Sunday funnies.

Franklin left this room untouched. There was no imprint of him upon its space. He kept his clothes out of sight, his work in the desk. In bed we came together as orderly as breakfast toast, patting each other on completion as one napkins the corners of one's mouth, sweeping the crumbs away to sleep. Had John not come along we might be thus retiring still.

John lays out newspaper to polish his daytime shoes. Brown Cordovan stain careless above the paleness of the carpet. He screws his exercise bar in the doorway to the bathroom. On the chaise, a muted seaweed silk, he piles the clothes that need to go to the cleaners, and throws his shirt there for Nancy to wash. John makes a boys' dormitory of my room.

At night Franklin went through things in order. His watch went on the nightstand, his tie on the tie rack. Love came in due time, after the house was locked and the lights were out. John eats up here if he is hungry, big sandwiches on a tray, ice cream melting in a bowl. Ready for me, he shuts the door and loves, TV and children still turned on downstairs. He oversleeps if he is tired; or if he has energy to spare he gets up at five o'clock to jog. Sometimes he likes his coffee while he shaves; sometimes he waits for it at work. John makes anarchy in my room.

Now, his motor churning, his shoes buffed, his mind on our kin, he chins to calm himself.

Harold is his anxiety. He hurts for this brother whose wife has left his bed. John is not a man to understand sleeping in a double bed with no one to share it. He may have doubts as to whether Harold, who has a hard time getting any project going, can find another wife—and Harold, being a minister, will have to have a wife.

John, not getting enough help from his chinning bar, turns to me for love.

"Is it all right?" he asks.

I tell him yes, wanting him.

It is as if he were reassuring himself with me that he will not meet his brother's fate, and he uses all his energies to dispel such a fear.

I go back, as I always do in love, to being sixteen on the beach; having my top at last untied, my pants at last pulled down. As my flesh grows soft under his hands and my wealth of hair gets between us in our kissing, John becomes for me the lifeguard on the beach. John, a reality, here, is a large happy fact above me. As he gives and takes the skin on his back grows tight as the hide on a drum, and the sounds of him are the sounds of being delighted. Beneath him my waves still come, and my eyes, opening, still makes stars. I lock my legs and find his tongue before I let him go.

Before he came to live with me I used to walk this room and chew my nails and twist my hair like a child who has lost a pet. I told myself, then, that what I felt for John was only lust disguised as devotion and that I would surely recover in time from such longing . . . Instead, I have grown to seek its each disguise.

Passion then, being clandestine, was easier to come by. In marriage it is more rare: in marriage the moat is harder to swim, the drawbridge is rustier, the castle is harder to scale.

Rolling over to lay my face against the sheet I am grateful for such times.

. . .

Comforted, his motor running slower, John is tender. He takes my tortoise brush and does the hundred strokes. In the live oak tree against our window birds sleep, and we have time to talk at last.

"This was some day," he says.

"Yes, Edward staying over."

He stretches out, confides, "This secretary isn't working out."

"Peggy?"

"It may be she will have to look for another place—"

We smile. All his Peggys sooner or later fall in love with him and have to leave. It's that way with a man like John.

I find a cotton gown, white like a schoolgirl's, and let him tell me about his brother.

Miserable, he reveals what he didn't say downstairs. "Velma walked out on him."

"How can you leave a preacher?" Meaning not how could you, but how is it possible to do so.

"It sure looks bad to the church."

"Is she tired of the extended family?" I remember that Velma hates parish life.

He registers the ultimate distress. "She's going off with someone else. A widower whom she met at church. That's the worst of it. I didn't want to say it all down there."

Velma, who has become my friend, dutifully made five children like her mother-in-law, and dutifully named them all good family names: Conrad, Gertrude, Hilda, Karl, and Max. Now by leaving she will have to troop them all, and their braces, and earaches, and piano lessons and DPT booster shots, over to disrupt a private solitary tryst with a widower from the church. Should I call to tell her to stay put, to advise her to leave the children with the mothers'-day-out program, assign her choir job to a new church member fresh from a junior college's *a cappella* choir, and get some stay-at-home grandmother to make coconut cakes for the bake sale while she slips off to love that widower in the lovely papered silence of his home. With a little coffee pot, some rooted flowers, and a daytime, sun-streaked, lumpy waiting bed, he would rise to her coming as he will never do across all those trikes and roller skates. Poor Velma: jumping from the frying pan, as she would say.

John says, "To do a thing like that to Harold. After fourteen years."

"We did a thing like that to Franklin."

He recoils, not wanting to be found in the wrong. "I didn't mean any harm to Hawkins. You would have left him anyway. And there was only little Frank. Harold has five." John tries to patch the past, distressed at having it reopened, forgetting that at the time his greatest hesitation was in taking "that little boy from his daddy."

"Yes, five is a lot more to lose." Conrad, Gertrude,

Hilda, Karl, and Max must be a comforting catechism for a man of cloth. "Will Velma take them?"

A shadow falls across his eyes. He doesn't like to think of this. "Harold thinks it wouldn't look right to fight for them, to try to get custody. We're going to talk about that tomorrow. It sure would help if Fred were still alive. He'd know what to do." A deeper shadow for this elder brother, gone.

"But Harold is doing all right?"

"Sure. You know Harold. He's going to be philosophical about it, see it in the best light. He loves the kids; he wants to do the right thing for the kids. He's not going to be bitter about it."

Poor Velma. I feel the weight from here of Harold not being bitter. At least Franklin, a gentleman through and through, was bitter.

"We're going to work it out this weekend, about the custody." John weighs it all, cracks his knuckles. "It helps that he's got the whole church on his side."

I can imagine the parsonage full of people commiserating with their pastor. This will be a comfort to the brothers Marshall; they like to deal from a full house.

Velma I met, as life makes coincidences, before I knew John, on a boat trip with Franklin to see the whooping cranes near the Rockport coast. We made a sultry ride through the marsh to glimpse—after the snowy egrets, the cormorants, the great blue herons—the awing presence of those large white birds standing silent in the grassy water's edge, becoming extinct.

Velma was the only other female who wasn't over sixty, Audubon, and wearing tennis shoes.

She was a small girl in blue jeans, very tired around the eyes.

"That your husband?" she asked.

"Yes."

"Just you two here?"

"Yes."

"Lucky. Last time I saw my husband alone was the week before our wedding."

Laughing, I asked the obvious. "After your wedding?"

"The honeymoon was a group affair. I guess we started the original commune. To be funny, ha, ha, Harold's four brothers, one is dead now, made reservations at our motel. There was this knock on the door at six o'clock in the morning and room service arrives with six orders of pecan waffles and six pots of coffee. Surprise. They all had a big laugh over that."

"Was it hard to get away to come here?"

"You can't believe how hard. But I schedule something once a year and send a big enough deposit so there is no backing out, not even if the District Superintendent comes, or the Bishop himself, or there's a Women's Society bake sale, or the Easter cantata for the choir. It's either that or get locked up for shock treatment."

"Franklin and I haven't much family. I have a brother, he has a sister."

"Jesus Holy Christ. Imagine."

I looked at Franklin, trying to see him answering that room service knock—such surprises were not a part of our ordered life—and felt envy for my newly made friend.

"What's your name?" she asked.

"Ellen."

"Mine's Velma." Like sisters, we gave each other given names.

Three years later, as John's new wife, I went to Houston to meet the clan, and there was Velma: tireder, pregnant, in an ancient tank-top dress.

"Jesus Holy Christ," she whispered in my ear, embracing me, a sister, squeezing me against her heavy bulge. "Imagine, you. Boy, did you jump from the frying pan."

John pulls me to him on the bed. "It's a real mess," he says, holding my hand for comfort. "There's never been a divorce in our family."

Which leaves me where I thought I was: outside the

family. It gives me additional empathy for my friend Velma. I let it go.

Wrapping me in a bear hug, John pleads, "I want them all to be happy."

"Maybe they are."

"How can you be happy if you're involved in a mess like that?"

I remind him that we thought we were happy in our rented room on a side street by the bridge, with pink cabbage roses on our wall.

He won't accept a parallel. "We knew it was temporary. I hated sneaking around like that, hated not being able to tell everybody. It was no good seeing you at all those parties and knowing we couldn't leave together."

"You married me so you could take me home."

"So no one else could."

"I wasn't what you'd planned." I ease things by reminding him of old stories.

"Right, I was after either the Sweetheart of the University or the Queen of the Tyler Rose Festival." He expands into his earlier self.

"Instead you got Rapunzel."

"I got the siren who sat in the water calling all the ships to wreck on the shore."

"Circe."

He furrows his brow as if to come up with a real answer. He likes to keep the record straight. "I guess I

married you because you make things grow. We didn't
have a garden; after work Mother didn't have time to
do much but cook, and cooking for that many took a
lot of time in our old kitchen. We never had things
inside the house like all these ferns or those big blue
things on the sunporch."

"Agapanthus lilies."

"That's how I could tell that you had flowers, you
used to call them all by name."

It is true that at those parties—with candles lit,
drinks flowing, crowds telling hunting jokes and football jokes and Aggie jokes—I did gravitate to what was
fresh and silent, automatically pinched off brown leaves
from my hostess's plants, delighted to stand where
hanging baskets spilled into a waterfall of vines. That is
how I spent my time before John: standing in the
greenery. And that is where he found me. "John, have
you ever met my wife? This is John Marshall—"

"What did you see in me?" he asks, settling himself
against me, needing to hear good things.

Inside the circle of his arms, for charity, I lie. "I
married you because you were a winner." As if any
woman in full possession of her mind would love a
winner, for they are never alone; they always travel
with a camp of followers and always watch to see that
you are voting for them.

But winners believe such apocrypha. Confident that
he has once again won the day, his brother sufficient to

the morrow, he shuts his eyes, instantly sleeping the sleep of the constitutionally sound.

With his ignition off, he looks as undisturbed as a yellow dog warming in the sun in a Mexican doorway.

I pat him between the ears. Good friendly John.

T W O

Friday, May 12

At breakfast the sky opens up and water falls in torrents, water that overflows creeks, blackens the sky, runs off into gullies, swells into flash floods. The rain that has at last broken through its dike of clouds now threatens devastation. Its coming is excessive, as our weather often is.

On TV we watch the news. Nearby towns are washing away, rivers are leaping from their beds, houses are being excavated and cars abandoned. There are reports of a dozen drowned.

Frank says, "We called DeWitt's mother, so she doesn't have to take the car pool. We're gonna ride our bikes."

"In this rain?"

"Some guys are going to try out their canoe. We wanta watch."

"Before school?"

There is shouting down the street; the sound of truancy. John tells him to be careful.

Ellen Nor lets her Bombay look out the back door; he understands monsoons.

I know the flash flood: once I saw a sheep, grazing

in a ravine, swept to death by a wall of water four feet high.

From the upstairs window of my room John and I watch the rain fall in sheets. Thunder seldom heard seems right above us on the hill. Thor avenging.

"Look at the boys, riding in it." We watch our bedraggled son race on slick streets.

"We used to do that back home," John tells me, "with no more sense than chickens standing in the rain, leaning back their heads and drowning. We all cut school."

"Frank said he has friends taking a canoe . . ."

"That's dangerous business; I heard that." He looks concerned. "It'll be as rough as riding rapids. I know about that." He stares outside, watches the storm. "The radio said, while I was shaving, that the low road had flooded over and been closed. That must be where they're going." He considers that. "I'll go by there on my way downtown."

John relates well to such adventures as taking the canoe. He has chased his share of firetrucks and waded in his share of swelling streams. It makes him good at sensing danger.

He will enjoy seeing where the road is cordoned off, getting out of his car and seeing the barricades. It will give him a chance to visit with the policeman and tell him of the time he and his brothers drove to Idaho, in a borrowed truck, to ride the rapids of the Snake River. John and the police will be buddies by the time the creek roars over its culvert into a cataract.

We talk of hurricanes, those plagues the ocean visits upon the coast, and of tornadoes, whose whirlwind funnels shamble little towns. Our weather brings fear when it gets out of hand.

I tell him about the sheep I saw, trapped by a wall of unexpected water.

"That wasn't on the coast."

"No. At my grandfather's farm. In Galveston we only worried about another flood."

Besides the image of the sheep, my mind is made uneasy by the weight of custody, which is the major burden of divorce. It is too grim to imagine having to call Franklin, or, worse, having John call Franklin, to say that we have let his one son drown. It is hard enough to be one parent; it is too much burden to carry the responsibility for two.

Last month we passed a motorcycle wreck. We were on our way out to dinner with Pete, the doctor friend who sniffles, so of course we had to stop. The boy's body was laid out flat in the street with arms outstretched, his face covered with a leather jacket, his head still in its star-embellished helmet. His Yamaha was jackknifed on the shoulder; the guilty car was parked unhurt beside it. Later, reading about the accident in the paper, I saw that the boy lived with his mother, that his parents lived apart. I tried not to think of that woman's phone call . . .

Sensing my concern, John says, "Don't worry about Frank. I'll check up on him." He kisses me against the rain-streaked pane, holding on until a new crash of thunder fades.

As suddenly as it came, the storm goes, spent, washing on down the river to flood other smaller streams.

Outside in the yard, in the fragrance of water, we catch our breath and watch the early birds. Usually up and gone by now, they have come back to feed again, wading in the rainsoaked lawn, shaking water from their feet like seagulls in the surf. They balance on delicate pencil legs.

John, almost to the car, turns back. "Would you like to go out to dinner?"

"With whom?"

"No one else. You and me."

"No brothers?"

He does not like my tone. "Karl and Max only stayed two days and nights."

"So they did. And Edward before that."

"Dress up, and we'll go get a steak."

"Promise no friends or relations? No comings or goings?"

"Promise."

I smile to let him know that pleases me. "Then I'll wear red and flowers in my hair."

. . .

Wearing red is an old lover's phrase.

We used it at a Christmas party when I was still hesitating, unable to make up my mind whether to meet him, whether to start the finish of my marriage to Franklin.

We were standing by a window seat heaped with silver tinsel-wrapped packages. The house was done in gold-sprayed cedar trees. Styrofoam circles intended to look like popcorn balls draped the mantle. Across the room, where Franklin was talking to a bank stockholder, were life-sized figures of a crèche in gold papier-mâché.

"I could find us a room," John had said, moving close so as not to be heard.

"I couldn't do that."

"Then come home with me."

"You know I can't." I turned my head. "Give me a little time."

"How will I know when you change your mind?"

"I'll be wearing red." I drew an A on my chest.

He was uneasy. "Will you have to think of yourself that way?"

"Of course. What do you think?"

"I think I wish we were in that room right now."

. . .

In the freshly laundered air I stay out back, on schedule. Mornings are for gardens.

My garden makes its own pattern through the year, moving through a round of seeding, potting, setting out, feeding, soaking, and blooming, to seeding again. It is a dependable frame of time: the yellow rose opens on its day as the larkspur does on another. It would be good if we could do the same—each one live by one's own time. As the layers of the earth shift by their own clocks, so do the crocuses bloom. I weed on Ellen time.

My garden, which was bone dry and now has flood plains in it, has been neglected in the week of brothers. I do remedial work: rebuild soil around roots uncovered by the rain, stake back the blooms the wind has flattened, pinch off dying leaves that need removing, prune bushes that have grown too crowded to branch out. I work gently in the wet dirt, not sure whose grave is in this loam, as careful as if uncovering a backbone from the past.

It will be good to have a night with John alone. We have had too much company here with his brothers arriving on the heels of my trip to Dallas, where, as I suspected, I was too much company for Laura Ann.

The nights Karl and Max were here they all talked of Harold long after I had climbed the stairs to bed.

John went comfortably from sitting up with my kin to sitting up with his. He enjoys company, especially when they move around from one room to the next, ending up in kitchen chairs having a second dessert. For much as the lawyers worried over their brother and his unfaithful departed Velma, they still found gusto enough to eat their way through half of my recipes. Nancy and I did chicken, beef, and shrimp in cheese, all very generously seasoned with chili peppers and spices. They even blessed their meals as a gesture to the absent preacher.

The strain of having them here was not in cooking for them; it was that they brought back too much of my past to me, parts of it that I do not want to go through a second time.

Serving the overgenerous meals around the clock took me back to schooldays at home during the long stretch of holidays spent feeding relatives. To the endless convoluted days at my parents' that turned on roasted turkeys with chestnut dressing, soft hot cornbread made and spooned at every meal, and stacks of chess and raisin-nut pies. These repasts were accompanied, in unvarying ceremony, with what my father ponderously pronounced to be good but not great wines.

At Christmas the house, decorated with velvet-bowed cedar boughs, was full of cooking smells and massed plants warming in winter pots by the window.

Kitchen trays of frosted plum cakes sat beside tin pie pans of African violets and ferns. We spent long evenings before the fire listening to my father talk, ending with the nightly ritual of Cognac from my grandmother's ruby-red cut glasses, and, on the right night, with the Bell Telephone Hour on the radio.

The mantle clock showed one time for them, another for me. For me, there were long hours to go before climbing the stairs to bed, for them there were only short hours away before they had more guests to feed. Our holidays were spent with my parents looking forward to this succession of seated meals, and with me wanting only for vacation to end, to be back in school, to catch sight of the lifeguard who worked the summer at the beach, to wait by my locker in case he walked by.

The brothers Marshall also took me back to my divorce.

They harped on that subject for hours as if I had no ears or feelings, as if it had no application to John. At every meal they went into long discussions over custody, over wrenching the children (Conrad, Gertrude, Hilda, Karl, and Max) from their kin. This was what I had also done to Frank: given him a new set of relatives to relate to, loosed old ties that have frayed with the years. They brought back to me my own losses, took me back to Franklin's mother's farm, her soft rushing voice talking of the men, the lazy rockers on her porch, the sheep fat by their forking riverbank, even her old wrinkled violet-scented cousins whom I will never press against my cheek again. John's brothers made painful to me the memory of the network of relations one divorces.

They also reinforced my guilt because I have cheated Frank out of what my parents gave me: a rooted union, one set on the limbing genealogy that is recorded for eight generations in a framed branching tree over Mother's bed.

To stand in my parents' house is to have the surety that one's parents' marriage is older than one's life, and created for it. In my earliest remembrance, their personalities were already set into the roles of mother and father, and these roles are the bond that holds their union together. Little remains of their separate identities as man and woman, and those are seen only as they serve the union. It is impossible to imagine my parents otherwise, responding to other partners.

My mother would be unable to go uncorseted, to serve some other man canned peas and frozen pies, and, for his sake, to let her garden run to weeds. No more could my father learn that rumps can be patted after office hours or that he could prefer a giggling woman with dyed-black hair and pushed-up bra to a second dessert and the late show on TV.

But the advantages of lifelong mating, like those of trust accounts, go to the next generation. Seeing what it cost my parents in daily interest to bend themselves to each other to make a union for me, I made a different choice.

And as a result I broke this continuity for Frank, giving him instead the embarrassment of uncles one must be introduced to, a funeral for a grandmother one has acquired at seven, a father one sees every other weekend—and a mother who was a woman first.

In this decision I got no help from home, either at the time or in my childhood.

My mother was not the best example of how to be a woman, as, through the years unable to get a response from my father, she pruned and mulched in compensation until she grew herself as dwarfed and mannered as a boxwood hedge.

My father did not deal directly with me, as if he had decided that a girl was a child you dealt with through a mother. Had he and I made contact, I might have learned sooner who I was, and done less damage on the way.

I tried to make contact with him, at least once, anyway. One Easter morning, when I was Ellen Nor's age, I made an offering to him, laying on his pillow what we at our house valued most, and he refused it. Or so the memory seems seen through the distortions of the past that a child's eyes give.

Easter—now a church time, when a cloth of white is on the altar and the scent of rose and lily is in the air

—was then centered on the masses of spring blooms in Mother's yard in which I hunted for Easter eggs, and where they hid them back for me to find again.

That Easter I went out barefoot in my nightgown to search for eggs before the sun was up. Finding none in the grass still beaded with dew, I tore up a fistful of my mother's prize dark tulips and an armful of snowy lilies. These I brought upstairs, their roots dragging dirt, to lay proudly on Daddy's pillow.

Had he hugged me, for the thought, or spanked me, for the uprooting, it would have taught me that love and touching are inseparable from the start. But he did not; such closeness was beyond him. "Here, hon," he said, half asleep, "let your mother see about these."

Mother explained that if one wanted to gather flowers for the house one asked first and then one carefully cut them with garden shears so that other blossoms would have a chance to grow.

She later made me hot cross buns, and told me we could plant some more that would grow back again.

But of course what I gave to my father had withered on the pillow of his bed.

It is good to have our company gone; I don't like to dwell so long in the past. I do better now.

Cutting cleanly, as my mother taught me, I take pinks and snaps and baby's-breath to vase, wanting to share a bouquet of newly opened colors from the rained-on garden with the antiquity of my house.

Inside, Ellen Nor is waiting, elephant in arm, to climb the morning to our hill.

The rain, soaking quickly through the clay, has all washed out of sight. Our white path is left steamed but somewhat dusty still. After a rain we find new fossils, washed into sight as rivulets cut down into this porous limestone formation that is the stuff of Carlsbads. Underground one can hear the roar of water cutting future caves; it is like walking high above the river Styx.

We find three gastropods tiny as cashew nuts, spiraled as a Dairy Queen, lying in a row like a triple grave in the clay. We find pelecypods as always, as plentiful as if they had been opened yesterday outside a beach café. Today the storm brings a new lead: the possibility of finding a blind salamander's jelly-coated eggs, which look like toy snakes in sticky plastic marbles. I push away the rocks where a flooded underground spring makes a small geyser at our feet. Ellen Nor beside me gets her tennis shoes sopping as we search in the warm rain-stream bubbling from the limestone.

The Texas blind salamander is a living fossil that spends its life, sightless and underground, dead-ended here on the Balcones escarpment. It has made the choice to renounce an amphibian's double life of day-lighting under pond frond and nightstalking for land prey. It has gone back home again to the water that its ancestor climbed out of fifty million years ago.

It is for me a creature of legend—like the little mermaid who gave up her life at sea for love, deformed her tail into legs, and tore her chest with air. In the same way I imagine that this salamander gave up all thought of land, of evolving into a dinosaur, even gave up her eyes and taste of air and feel of land for someone who could not leave the water. And there she has stayed with her legs no longer required for swimming, her color not needed for camouflage, her shovel-head becoming as transparent as the artesian wells she lives in.

Such blind alleys are easy to relate to. Who knows but that the human species is one: an anachronism without a tail, without gills, a coconut-headed hairless slow-runner, ill adapted to two legs.

Ellen Nor and I get wet and love it. The edges of our jeans get soaked as we talk of salamanders. She likes the word, wants to call her beast Sally Mander. Our friend, Sahib from Bombay, rolls down his beaded eye at this, disapproving, as I try to explain that this is not a proper name for him. To me it would be like naming a frog Pachy Derm.

We talk of names like these, and other general names. I try to give her some idea of genus, phylum, class, and order. My timing is inappropriate; a four-year-old is more concerned with possession than with classifying. I know this, but I am anxious that she not be limited in her scope, that she not be confined to quilting, weeding, or digging like her forebears. Her future is our future, all of ours, and in my heavy-handed, shovel-headed way I want to open all the world to her.

I came back from Dallas last week with new resolve in this direction: our visit to Laura Ann did not provide us with a good example of a grown-up girl.

Edward's wife is the Princess of her parents' expectation. She still has the air of pleasing that goes with walking down the runway, a glowing Bluebonnet Belle. The tulle dress from her senior dance must still be hanging at her mother's. As was expected of her, she chose from all her suitors a tall, dark knight in scrubsuit. The trouble is that happily-ever-after is a country run by husbands, away from the footlights.

My conviction is that girls who know the right spells to cast can get out of their own towers without waiting for some passing prince.

I wish I had known the right words to use at my brother's house. My visit there, which put a hex on all of us, turned, as life does, upon an egg.

Ellen Nor had ridden to Dallas, seat-belted, in the back, drawing pictures of her elephant on sheets of typing paper with thick red and blue felt markers.

Finding us isolated together in the car, Edward switched off the radio to talk. "How do you like being a mother? Going on the second decade?"

"In small doses."

"It doesn't look that way. The store you set by her." He looked in the mirror at his niece.

"She is the human race. After all . . ."

"What egotism for your genes."

"What responsibility."

"It's sport to watch the making of a mother. As a scientific phenomenon. It's one thing to read up on the symptoms as described in medical journals: carrying children's pictures, identifying with the young as extensions of oneself . . . But to have the chance to observe a mother, live, in her natural habitat—"

"Why pick on me, you had one of your own."

"But you're a more impartial study; I don't owe you my life."

"Don't use me as a model; I don't have many answers."

"No chance of that." And then, more seriously, he added, in a bitter tone, "It looks like you can take that either way."

He let the radio play awhile, hurtling up the highway ten miles over the speed limit, letting towns put distance between us. Then, "How are things with John?"

"He's a friendly man."

"I want things to get on between you two."

"And I."

"I like him."

"I like him, too."

We paused on that.

After another town he asked, "What has become of old Franklin? The Discarded."

"I wave out the window when he brings Frank home." A bad answer, which is the truth.

"Obviously you're not on speaking terms enough to switch it so my nephew could come along with us."

"It is already set up, every other Friday—"

"Frank could have toured the hospital with me. Who knows, with a little exposure to bedpans he, too, might long to join this select profession."

"Don't heap guilt on me, Edward, about Frank."

"Why not? You thrive on guilt."

"My Protestant ethic. I was born into sin."

"Your uptight parents; you were born to them."

"Don't play shrink, you don't have the empathy for it."

"Think how fitted I would have been at it, instead of taking the stethoscopic Fifth Amendment."

"Being in internal medicine suits you; you will learn to divide and conquer the organism."

"You're an unpleasant person for a sibling." He swerved around a truck.

As I say, we get on well alone.

We drove in silence until we hit the Dallas expressway at lunch hour. Ellen Nor woke from a nap on her sheets of typing paper and climbed between us in the front seat, needing to go immediately to the bathroom at the height of the noon traffic. "My mother," she told Edward, "lets me go at the filling station any time I need to." She was cross with him, not being as fond of uncles as Frank is.

"Your mother is too lenient on the future of the race," he explained. "You may have to wet your pants because I'm not going to stop."

I slept badly in the visitor's daybed at my brother's duplex. The crowded rooms there had an atmosphere I was not accustomed to, as if all the boundaries would move with a push of the hand, like biscuit dough. It was too soft and yielding an environment for me.

Breakfast made it worse. For over thirty years of weekdays I have breakfasted on wholewheat toast and eggs, with Sundays saved for something hot and homemade. That first morning at Laura Ann's, my brother, raised at the same table as I was, had raspberry Toast-'ems and grape Pop Tarts. There was no bacon, no eggs in sight. In our glasses we had something called Tang, which tasted like warm flat filling-station orange soda pop.

The afternoon was long. After two Cokes and some Funyions, Laura Ann got out of her gown and robe into some plaid shorts and a pullover to wait for Edward. Her legs were rounded, her dimpled knees slightly bent, in the stance of a girl leaning back to shift the heavy weight of a full-term baby. It was a wishful posture. She padded about in scuffs as if very pregnant, hitting her heels first; her large melon breasts looked swollen and ready to nurse. From time to time, as the afternoon went by, as she jiggled the ice in her Cokes, tears crowded the blue-shadowed corners of her eyes.

When Ellen Nor told her, "My mother lets me play outside the house," she opened the door to show my daughter the small unfenced yard. There, predictably, Ellen Nor found a small neighbor boy who called her over to watch him urinate into his sand castle. When he tried to bury a resigned Bombay in the same, Ellen Nor retaliated by shoving him into the sand on his face. After that they got on fine.

"I used to have a friend who was a tomboy like that," Laura Ann said wistfully.

"Did she turn out all right?" I asked, not sure at all if we could agree on what would be called all right.

"Gee, I don't know. I lost track." She looked vague

about this friend of hers who didn't go to camp and college and walk down the runway with roses in her arms, and who was now forgotten.

When Ellen Nor was brought in for her nap she decided that she was big enough this trip to take it in the baby bed in its clean blue and white room. By herself she climbed into the Mother Goose crib, beside which a painted chest of drawers, full of baby garments, waited. Laura Ann had brightened the nursery with a pot of yellow daisies on the window sill and a music box that played *Lullaby and Goodnight*.

Edward came home at last and had a handful of the onion-flavored cornmeal snacks with two martinis. With his metal shaker in hand, he looked for all the world like a doctor on daytime TV. After supper, Laura Ann said to me in the kitchen, "I'm really sorry it took so long. Ed always tells me what a great cook you are and how organized you are." I apologized for myself and for my brother's lies. Off schedule, hating gin, I retired after a decent interval to my daybed in the back, leaving them alone to wish that I were gone.

The second morning, having tossed all night like the Princess on the pea, and beginning to worry because Laura Ann was still bleeding intermittently and Doctor Kildare was doing nothing, I asked if I could have an egg for breakfast.

"Sure, I guess we've got some. Sure." Laura Ann sounded uncertain. Edward had been gone since five in the morning and had left no instructions for me or her if things should get worse. She looked around the shelves as if looking for an oddity—oregano or thyme —and then remembered and opened the refrigerator. She didn't have an egg.

It was too much. There was no more glue to hold herself together. Too much pressure and nothing she could do. "I guess I forgot at the store. I'm not very careful since it doesn't seem to matter what I eat . . . for the baby . . . I'm losing it again anyway . . ."

On and on she cried, chewing in her fingers, keeping her eyes shut tight, trying to close all her orifices against this most awful reality. Then, as if to keep pace with her crying, her bleeding began in earnest. At this I decided Edward could come home, although Laura Ann was hesitant for me to call him, she being a stubby child who was trying to do right. As I had thought before, children should not have children.

Relaying a message in the hospital was a long process which created the impression that unavailability had been built into the Hippocratic oath. I wrapped a blanket around my sister-in-law, who said, "Sorry, really . . . It's been the most awful . . . Momma and Daddy couldn't come down. And Ed is never . . . Here all by myself all day . . . I tried so hard to keep it . . ." Her cheeks were wet. Her blouse was wet.

With one hand she held my hand, and, with the other, she clutched the blanket, like Ellen Nor holding onto her beast.

When Edward got home I was trying to find nutmeg and brandy for hot milk, which seemed to me a better idea than the tranquillizer he gave her.

He blamed a lot on me, as I was handy, and strong enough to blame. "She's tried to hold it back since you've been here. Maybe your coming made this worse. You scare her to death, never showing anything. I told her you can't help it, that you're just like that. She thinks you don't care that she's losing it. She thinks you're being critical all the time."

But it may have been that he was projecting all his judging ways on me. I call her sister; he's the one who calls her failure. "John's idea was not too good," I said, confirming what we had known from the start.

"You're right about that, Rima. Fly on off."

"I'll get us to the airport by myself."

He made no argument to that, as his mind was already on the reality that his wife must have an ambulance. In parting, he laid one more piece of blame on me. "What on earth made you think of giving milk to someone who's nauseated?"

"I didn't think." Perhaps I had mother's milk on my mind.

"Tell John I may be back down soon."

"He'll still be saving Harold."

"Tell Frank it's his turn next. When things get settled up here."

"He'd like that; he was glad to see you."

"Can you hand me that damned blanket?"

"Take care of her, Edward."

Now Laura Ann is pregnant no longer. I imagine her sitting, weeping, in the blue-painted room, trying to decide when to start again to make another baby. In the meantime she will have to keep the duplex clean and serve my brother his preformed breakfasts that pop from cardboard boxes. She will write letters to her Momma who can't come down because of her Daddy's bad back. Her Daddy will feel too low to write.

If I were her mother I wouldn't wish my daughter to be where Laura Ann is.

"We need to eat." Ellen Nor conveys her stomach's time.

"I was thinking about Edward's Laura."

"They had a big sandpile in this boy's yard. A big sandpile that he pushed my Bombay in."

"Yes, that's true."

"Bad boy."

We gather up our shells and start down the hill.

Ellen Nor makes one more observation. "Uncle Ed's Laura bites her fingernails."

"Will you do that?"

She inspects her blunt fingers. "They got all dirty looking for Sally Mander."

"See that they stay that way." Bluebonnet Belles don't have dirty hands.

We get a treat after our girls' lunch. John calls me to sign some papers on the farm. Every family has a piece of land they should have kept until prices rose, or kept acres they should have sold before the prices dropped. Every family is one bad transaction away from real money, and my father's was no exception. From time to time, to try to make amends, we parcel out another section of what remains of my grandfather's farm.

So few times have I dressed for men in the daytime since I was married that as I put gloss on my lips, rebrush my hair, and change from pants into a sleeveless belted dress with a row of round white buttons down the front, I feel the same suspense, the same churning in my stomach, as when I used to ready myself to meet John in that papered room. Inside that door there was always a moment of silence before we crossed the space to each other, a moment of looking that was almost more real than what came after.

There was also such a deliberate dressing-up when I made my slow, resolute trip downtown to ask Franklin for a divorce. Even the same silence as we looked across his carpeted office, appraising each other, before he said, "Ellen, this is unexpected. Did you have an errand in town?"

But this trip today is not for such encounters. Today I arrive as John's wife and we all talk at once, for I have a daughter with me, and he has a secretary who is as friendly as her boss.

To me, who does not know her well, Peggy seems typical of all the girls John has hired before: she has a bright air, puffed blond beauty-shop hair, and the sort of standard curvy figure that seems very conscious of itself.

"She sure is cute," she says of Ellen Nor. "He sure is busy," she brags on John, who is admired by all the Peggys whom he employs.

When he comes out to greet us, the secretary offers to look after Ellen Nor. "She can stay with me; I'd just love to watch her."

"She might like to use your typewriter," I suggest.

"Why, that'd be fine. Here let me move this pile of stuff." She shoves four copies of a lengthy brief aside as if it were only a letter she was writing home. She gives my daughter her attention, understudying John; she thrives as he does on their visitors.

As we go into the office Ellen Nor picks out her name while Peggy leans out of the way in her chair, swinging her foot and humming a tune. She watches the little girl through lashes weighted with mascara.

The legal conveyance of land does not take long; I read over the papers, then sign my name in the presence of a notary brought in from down the hall. In John's leather client's chair I feel at home. I cannot imagine coming to this cluttered office with its shelves of books and walls of gold-framed diplomas and certificates to ask for a divorce. This is a comfortable room in which to play the role of wife.

After our business, John takes us on the customary tour that Ellen Nor expects. He lets her take her time. In the conference room she tests each leather chair, Three Bears style, and selects the one at the head of the table. In the file room her daddy writes out a copy of her legal, downtown name: Ellen Maitland Marshall, and, below it, her daily name. These he Xeroxes on seven sheets of thin, pink manifold, and gives them to her for a souvenir.

As we are leaving, John reminds me, "We're going out tonight."

"I'm wearing red, remember?" I thank him with a smile.

The secretary joins in brightly. "Have you got a new dress, Mrs. Marshall?"

"Pants. They're not really new, as clothes go."

"Oh, I just love pants suits—I mean to work in, too. They're so comfortable, aren't they?"

"Thank you for watching her."

"She sure is cute," she says. "Bye, now, Eleanor, you be sure to come back. Goodbye, Mrs. Marshall."

She has made going to John's office seem a trip through the Looking Glass, where reality is altered: we became older and smaller than we are in the outside world.

Ellen Nor punches the elevator button, descending us to the ground like Alice going down the Rabbit's hole.

I am jealous of the Peggys, in spite of myself. That is because they keep a husband's time; they are the alloters of his day. They know that three fifteen is insurance adjusters, and four o'clock is deed of trust; they know when to remind their boss, "You have an eleven o'clock appointment with Mrs. Smith." Their day turns on these tick-tock priorities, with the precision of a school day. Coffee comes, like recess, at ten and two. They learn when to file the yellow sheet and when to mail the onion skin . . . They wind the clocks of men that wives only sleep with.

Yet I couldn't do that: set myself by another's second hand. I would not like to spend my life moving someone else through Central Daylight Saving Time. The world I am accustomed to, of quilts and flowers and fossils, such self-employments, turns at a speed one sets oneself. This seems a small but valuable autonomy.

As Through the Looking Glass, the unexpected becomes the expected, the unplanned the reason for the descent, the past becomes the present, and the present, past. A world in which I used to live waits for us at the corner.

"Hello, Ellen."

We face each other at a red light. Stopped. "Franklin, hello." I offer him back a handshake that I owe.

"This is little Ellen?"

"Yes."

When she shows him her name on seven sheets of manifold, he says solemnly, "Hello, Ellen Nor."

She approves the proper way he divides her name.

"You've been to his office?"

"Yes." We are talking of John.

He addresses my daughter, "May I buy you a donut?"

"Who are you?"

Belatedly, awkwardly, I introduce him. "This is Frank's daddy, Mr. Hawkins."

"I like chocolate-covered donuts, Mr. Hawkins."

"Perhaps your mother would make an exception in her diet and have one too." He looks at me. "At least a cup of coffee, Ellen."

How well he knows me; he wouldn't offer Toast-'ems. "Yes, coffee."

It is inevitable to be caught together at a light. We had treaded long enough the length of court-ordered time, coexisting, with him picking Frank up at school on his Fridays and honking as he brought him home on Sundays.

It has been a space of years long enough that we can ask, I hope, "How is it with you?" and not mean in the bed, in my case, or living all alone, in his.

He looks thinner; his clothes hang looser than I remember. His shoulders seem slightly rounder. The faint lines around his mouth are etched deeper now, and there is the beginning of a shadow under his eyes. These do not detract: he is a handsome man, pencil slim. His face is tighter, though, more closed. He is controlled, though gracious, as he orders two chocolate-covered donuts and two cups of coffee, black. He assumes the liberty of remembering.

"You're wearing your hair down," he says.

"It's the style at last. Straight."

"I didn't expect such a resemblance." He watches my daughter smear her face with chocolate.

"A graven image." He knows I do not kid.

"How is it, having a girl?" We had talked of one, ourselves.

"More complex."

"Frank seems to get on with her."

"Better than with me."

"He speaks well of you."

"You know he doesn't mention me to you at all." I smile, expecting us to be honest at the least. We can't go back to being strangers.

He smiles, too, but only with his mouth. His eyes are still observing, noncommittal. "Silence I take as speaking well."

He intends a small stab here, I'm sure—implying that he had once taken my silence as a sign that all was well when I was leaving him. It is his way to never give words away outright. Sharp-tongued, he edges them to cut both ways.

I tell him about our son. "He rode off in the pouring rain this morning."

"How are things at his school? The riots?" He keeps track. I remember that he did this before, as if he had a folder on both of us, with entries noted and dated. As now he must clip from the paper school items to discuss on every other Friday.

"I don't know." I feel as if I were apologizing. "It is hard to keep your eye on each silting of the river."

"The overview. You haven't changed." He knows this about me from before, having remarked many times that on all matters I tend to see nothing between a single classified shell and the epoch it was trapped in. My sense of time, as he used to observe, is not germane to the real world.

Being with this man who is not my husband is like taking a weight off my shoulders; it is such relief to be clearly seen again. I tell him, "You know I have that problem. But it does seem so obvious that there will be fights and discord, that it will not be amicable for a good long time."

"That is not much help to Frank, is it?"

"No, I don't help." You do that for me, on your weekends with him.

After a pause, "How are you getting on?" He is asking about John.

"Well." I find the right word hard to select.

"And how is your brother?" He moves on.

"He asked about you."

He smiles with his eyes. "I can imagine." He did not care for Edward. "You two still as close?"

I had forgotten that he begrudged my tug with Edward, seeing it, as John does not, as a sign of intimacy. "We still fight," I say, giving him the answer that he was looking for. "Laura Ann lost another baby. This was her third. Do you remember?" He was there for the first, which seems a long time ago.

"He will have his way, won't he?" He used to say the same of me, and not just when I wanted free. He used to tell us that the mainline Maitlands always gave themselves the biggest slice.

"He hasn't changed in that. Nor I." A fact he does not need to be told.

"Passing it on, I see." He observes the sticky end of donut two. He also comments on my daughter's hundred-dollar pet.

My coffee grows cold with sitting. Franklin orders another cup for me, instructing the waitress to pour the old one out. He is still proprietary: assuming that I want it hot. That hasn't changed; what has changed is that it doesn't seem as bad.

"You act as if you own me," I had said in some parting dialogue.

"I give the same care that I expect in return; that's fair."

"What you call fair is counting, one for you and one for me, eye for an eye, and tooth for a tooth." I was comparing him in my mind to John's openhandedness.

"Yes, I measure things. That is my job, to keep a fair account." Then, he had added, "How else could I value you correctly?"

My second cup half done, I ask, "How is it with you?" It is unexpected how much I care to know.

"Well, thank you." Just slightly mimicking, he gives back my reply to me.

I wait, letting that go.

"I'm dating." He flushes as he uses such an adolescent word. It is clear he thinks of it in other terms: "I have a woman now, Ellen."

"Who?" I should be pleased for him.

"A teacher." He isn't giving anything away. As was his habit, he forces me to make the next move.

"I'm glad." I smile, because I'm not glad, because he knows it, because he's forced me into lying. It was a chess game living with this sharp-minded man.

He feigns surprise, "But Frank must have told you? He has met Babs several times."

He has won, of course, as he can tell from looking at me. He knows that my son does not confide in me.

I concede the game. "No, of course he hasn't, Franklin. But then, I take his silence as boding well for you."

He gives me a nod for that. "Give your mother my regards when you go down for your birthday."

"She'll be pleased I saw you."

He accepts that; he knows she thought him a gentleman. She also thought him right for me—in the way that mothers have of seeing what you don't.

We shake hands, both of us this time, at the corner. In some ways opponents are closer than lovers.

As I watch his back go down the street I seem to watch myself disappear. If Franklin was a mirror for me, it must be that I didn't like the sight. He showed too clearly a woman out of step with time, dependent on her brother, greedy, which is a sure description of my daughter also. Franklin is right; I pass it on.

"We don't live with Frank's daddy." Ellen Nor tells me. It is not a question, although I sense one that she cannot put into words.
"No."
"We live with my daddy."
"Yes."
"You like my daddy best?" This time it is the question, as she pulls on me, her face wide open for my answer.
"I do. I love your daddy."
Love. From what fairy story came the myth that love entitled us to take what we want. That love allowed us to hack at other lives. That love could be made the excuse for rounding the shoulders of a fair and measured man. It was my decision that love would make a pride of children, both with different names, to spoil the genealogy, and hurt the heart.

Before I dealt in love I dealt in order, which was more dependable. We always had our coffee by the window. You could set your metronome by the time we took our wholewheat toast. Just at the cooling of the day, no later, no sooner, we fixed a drink and walked the garden path, making shadows in the dusk. We observed at each time of year where our shadows fell; we made notes of the setting of the winter sun and summer sun. We patterned our house and yard as neatly as a quilt, stitching each square's design in by repetition, until we made a patchwork of the whole.

Franklin taught me that if one has trouble with the arbitrary length decreed by humankind's biology, it helps to know the breakfast egg has boiled three minutes today and will do the same tomorrow.

It was Franklin who kept unaltered my birthday pilgrimage, who understood its significance to me.

On our first trip home after we were married, Mother had planned a special cake and corraled some cousins, home from Sophie Newcomb, for a party. Franklin and I stayed at a motel, so as not to put Mother out. He, a new son-in-law and a proper guest, had brought Mother an illustrated book on plant diseases. He talked to my father of the unsold farm and made some helpful suggestions for combining acreage and reinvesting the proceeds. They were very pleased with him.

But I had not come to see them; I had come to see the summer beach. "Today I am one year older," I told Franklin, wading out to meet the tide.

"That is a passage of time you understand—your own."

"But it wouldn't be my birthday somewhere else."

"Have you never been gone?"

"Not this day. I'm like the water fowl who have to migrate back."

"Have you ever seen them at Rockport, at the preserve?"

"No. I only come here."

"We'll have to go."

"Not on my birthday."

"No, in the spring. I can see that this coast is a landmark you need to count on."

But by the time of the divorce I found Franklin's invariability to be rigidity. With John to compare him with, I faulted Franklin for all those things that I had needed most.

"You've set our lives up so we can go through all the motions without having to relate at all. Getting to you in the midst of this stifling routine is like trying to get to you through your mother at the farm." We were fighting a week after I had told Franklin that I wanted out; but at the same time, because we always ate out on Sunday nights, we were dressing to keep a dinner reservation.

"We spend all our time at home together." Franklin thought that wives tended to feel neglected.

"But you have prearranged it all. We could be robots for all the contact that we've had."

"Didn't we say it gives a certain security to follow a routine?"

"Security, that's all you bankers think of. I'd rather eat crumbs in a rented room."

"I doubt you will for long," Franklin had said dryly. He was not misled by my reference.

"I can't get through to you—"

Franklin put on his suit coat, as time was running out. He helped me zip my dress, and handed me a sweater to wear against the restaurant's air-conditioning. We started out the door on schedule as he finished the conversation. "I meant to be a clock to you, Ellen."

Mirror, mirror on the wall, who is most foolish of them all.

Downtown is crowded with shoppers who hurry along burdened with bundles of camp clothes and graduation gifts. Nearby store windows show both wedding gowns and nosegayed sheets and towels for the bride.

Too many cars honk in our direction. Ellen Nor takes my hand and navigates the intersection. We cross the wider street almost hit by twenty cars, the young leading the unseeing.

Solicitous, she asks, "Did you get dirty in your contact lenses?"

"No. I am crying in the middle of the main street because I am a fool."

"Because you love my daddy most?"

"Because I love your daddy most." Ellen Nor is wise beyond her years.

"Uncle Ed's Laura bites her fingernails," she offers.

"What a good idea." I try it out across the stampede of traffic.

Going home we hear on the radio that a boy has drowned, his motorcycle swept down in the deluge this morning. My heart goes out to his parents. He was Frank's age; too young to be riding a Kawasaki 750. His sand ran out in little more than half a score.

When someone dies it breaks the sound barrier of the day; you hear the crash of trivia, the clap of the ordinary in all its force. Time is never the same, arranging itself into Before and After.

Divorce, a smaller death, is in this way the same. Before seems someone else's diary, trite, an embarrassment, overdone and oversaid. All of that forgotten, put away and stored, a piece of stale wedding cake, an iceberg out of sight beneath the deceptive lake of After.

The air is clear; the early flood forgotten. It ravaged like a wolf descending on the fold, taking its sheep, leaving. Grazing continues as it had before—there is some blood on the grass, some fleece in the wind.

It is with relief that I see Frank lock his ten-speed to a tree when we are home, and Ellen Nor is napping. He takes his time coming in. It isn't until he faces me that I see why. His nose is a bloody mess. Peering at him I feel like a movie camera zooming in for a closeup shot of violence. I am looking at what is very painful to see: his face wears both clotted blood and a look of disbelief.

"What happened, Frank?"

"I got beat up, is all." He thinks my question obvious.

He lets me hold an icepack to his nose. He is outraged—that it should be *his* nose. It is unjust. "I treat them better than anybody in the whole advisory."

Them. "Who?"

"It was LeRoy who did it. Him and White Hog. Two of them . . . Three if you count him jerking out my chair." He grinds his fist in his eyes, the enormity of three attackers bringing tears. "The teacher calls him Charles." He mimics, "Char-uls, don't let me see you do that a-gain. We all have to act the same in this classroom." For a minute he forgets and is on the side of the teacher. "They call him White Hog. Him and Billy Jo follow LeRoy around." His voice rises to a pitch of distress. "What are you supposed to do when somebody puts his knuckles in your face and somebody else jerks your chair, and," here his voice crescendos, "somebody takes your Social Studies paper and wipes his feet all over it?"

"You might tell somebody that his head is almost as fat as his ass."

"Mo-ther!" He gets up and holds his own icepack. Towering and bloody, and very insulted, by them and by me, he protests, "You sure aren't any help."

"No, that's the way with mothers." Franklin said that very thing.

"I couldn't call them stuff like that. They'd kill me."

"What do you call those boys, Charles, LeRoy, Billy Jo?"

"What do you think?" He is upset with me, not meaning to be the one accused. "I know those names you aren't supposed to call them."

"Do you? Do you know the first one is 'them?' "

"After they got me, and I told the teacher, and she sent us to the counselor, then the dumb counselor didn't do anything but send us all to study hall. That was really dumb. I had to sit at the same table with them making cracks about me for a whole hour."

Good counselor. I can guess the comments whispered at that table: LeRoy saying, loud enough to be overheard, "That Frankie is just a egg; he is snow white on the outside but he just yellow on the inside."

Frank wants to be defended. "Dad will do something about it when I call him. He'll know what to do. That dumb teacher didn't even send me to the nurse."

"Yes, your father will want to hear." This is as good a time as any to open up another wound. As offhand as I can manage, I say, "When I saw him downtown today, he asked about the riots at your school."

"No kidding? Did he?" He is glad to hear that. A flush rises across his face that makes his nose look redder still: he looks remembered.

"And will you call John, too?" I ask.

He hesitates, not sure where his allegiance lies, not certain of the importance of a nose. He hedges. "If I get time. Grayson's coming over—"

"Does he know about your fight?"

"Sure." Proudly. "They all know. It was all over school. Me, and the guy who drowned."

"Did you know him?"

"Yeah. Sorta. He stole that 750."

"Does that matter?"

"He didn't even have a license to ride it. I mean, he wasn't near old enough, even."

"Did your friend's canoe make it all right?"

"They almost got it too. It dumped over and they nearly got washed under the bridge."

"Water is dangerous." It can't be contained on its rare visits. "Did the storm make any trouble at school?"

"No, I told you, *they* made trouble." And we are back at the beginning.

Almost to the telephone, he asks in a very casual tone, "Hey, Mom, how come you saw Dad?"

"We ran into him downtown. He bought coffee for me, and two donuts for Ellen Nor."

"That baby. I bet she made a mess."

"He thought she did." I don't like to further separate him from his father.

He blurts it out. "He tell you he has a girl named Babs?"

"Yes. He said she was a teacher."

"She teaches over at college and speaks three languages. And, boy, is she pretty." He is obviously relieved to get this off his chest at last.

There is not much that I can say to that. I smile, so he won't feel he shouldn't have told me, and remind him of matters at hand. "I bet your nose will really swell tonight."

He lays down the icepack and touches his opened face. The blood has dried; it leaves none on his fingers and that is disappointing. "Dad will tell me what to do," he says. "I wish this was his Friday." He picks up the receiver.

Not wanting to hear a one-way talk with Franklin, I go out to the sunporch to check the plants for water. The scheffelera droop. I should have set them out so they could soak up the minerals in the rainwater.

I know Frank misses living with his father. It always works out that mothers get the child, because mothers are home, and fathers, if they are lucky, get a few weekends and a vacation in the summer.

Going up to the farm to his grandmother's is not the same for a boy as having a father knock each evening at the same time and stick his head in to say goodnight. Frank must miss that bedtime ceremony, which ended when he was six. For all John's affection, it is not the same. Now Frank helps his father court a girl who knows more languages than she needs to talk to him. Before too long he may get to wake "that baby" at another house. He may have half-sisters all over town (although it is impossible for me to believe that Frank would be as related to a sister kin to him by sperm as to a sister kin through a common womb).

I do not like to think of him with Franklin and a new wife, any more than I like to dwell on Franklin's response to this teacher whom Frank describes as pretty. When I left I told Franklin that an attractive man like he was would surely find some nice girl he could love before too many years went by.

So carelessly do we place the curse upon ourselves.

Karol has had a crappy morning and accepts a beer. "You can only drink so much coffee before your palms begin to sweat. My neck feels hairy. It's nerves. Nookie

coming over tonight, I guess. Franklin County, Jr.,
showed me where they beat him up."

"He showed me, too."

"Who is he talking to? Some more of the gang?"

"I think to Franklin."

"Oh, sure. Not bad to have two daddies to get a little
sympathy from. And I don't have to guess which one
he called first." She drinks her beer, making a face,
wishing it were stronger and she not due back at work.
"Did you hear about the boy who drowned?"

"Yes. He was overturned in the flash flood."

"I heard that he stole that motorcycle."

"Does that matter?" I ask for the second time. She
and Frank think retribution, as if they think death can
be faced if one has stolen a vehicle, because the con-
verse means that if you don't steal one you won't get
killed. This evades the truth that a black bean awaits us
all; that we are all thieves, in our own way.

"It sure was some storm. Only Texas gives you all
four seasons of the year, every month. We get drought
and then we get monsoons."

"The birds could tell it wasn't sprinkler water; they
came back a second time to feed."

"Maybe the chlorine gets to them, too. My tap water's worse than a swimming pool."

"Think how many eons it must have rained to make
the oceans at the start."

"You think about it—that's more up your alley."

She shakes her empty can, nervous still. She is keyed up for a date with the man who sells warehouses.

We talk about her daughters, and her mother.

Frank comes in, his phoning apparently completed. He looks around, glad to have an audience. "Karol, did you get a good look at my nose?"

"I faint at the sight of blood."

"It isn't bleeding." He sounds let down. As he talks to us he keeps an eye out for the door; he does not want to get caught with us when Grayson arrives. Peers and mothers strain the loyalties.

"What did your daddy say?" Karol pumps him for a little gossip.

"He said I could transfer to another school if I wanted to, a private school or something. Or we could go talk to the counselors about getting me in a better advisory. He said it was up to me, that he'd go with me if I wanted him to. I may not stay at this pig school; I'm deciding."

Karol looks at me. "What did I tell you? That's Franklin, taking action. Like I told your mother, Frank, when Sally Surrey gets raped, I want Franklin there."

"Witnessing or participating?" I ask.

"Mo-ther—"

"Getting outraged, at least."

I admit, "He does know the niceties of revenge."

"Exactly. When to lynch and how."

Frank repeats, to get the conversation back to him. "Well, he said I could transfer if I want to—" He hears his friend and starts toward the kitchen. "Listen, I gotta go."

Karol offers him a positive word. "Maybe they'll pick on someone else tomorrow."

"Fat chance of that," he says.

"Where are you going?" I ask the question mothers need to ask.

"Over to Brewster's. We're going to mess around. His mother's fixing pizza. I hope I can eat it with this face."

"Be home before it's dark."

"Before it's dark?" He looks insulted at this, on top of the indignity of his fight. Over his shoulder we hear his muttered, "Crap."

Karol looks pleased.

Watching her tear at a nail, I decide to confide. "I had coffee with Franklin today."

"You did? Where?"

"Downtown. I ran into him on the street."

She looks full of sympathy. "That must have been a strain. Wasn't it?"

"Some."

"It's bound to be. It always is. I used to take a tranquillizer every time Bob Surrey showed his face."

"Now you take one for your mother."

"But it's five milligrams instead of ten." She narrows

her eyes, woman to woman. "Did you wish you were back with him?"

"Some."

"You're bound to. I know how that is; they can always get a hook into you somewhere. How did he look? I never see him."

"Thin."

"Say, you do sound bothered."

"Bothered because it made me feel guilty."

"They really know how to do that."

They. Ex-husbands. But Franklin was *we* for eight years of marriage and two before that. He was *we* for a decade and you can't entirely let that go, not the length of ten birthdays.

Karol stays positive. "Well, cheer up. It's over. It was bound to happen sooner or later. Before you know it you'll be having him in for drinks."

With Babs and a bilingual baby on her lap? "Not yet."

"Well, it will come, you'll see. Bob Surrey and that whore send me embossed two-dollar Christmas cards every year." She heads for the back door. "It's time to Fly United—that's the Siamese twins' motto."

Sticking her head back through the screen she gives me her real news. "Black Nancy said her daughter had a fight at school yesterday. I forgot to tell Frank."

"Was she hurt?"

"You better believe she was doing the hurting. She

admitted it herself, Nancy said. She told Nancy right out that she scratched some white girl's face with her fingernails in the restroom and the principal couldn't open the door to break it up because it was the girls' bathroom. You know they grow those awful fingernails."

Good news to hear that some girls are fighting. Maybe there will be mutation from passivity for girls after all. The ones at the bottom of the pecking order may use their hands as weapons to claw their way to the top. The rest of us could learn from that. "Tell Nancy I'm proud."

"You tell her Monday. She and I don't talk about it any more than we can help. We're both scared to death. This morning we both fell apart over the vacuum cleaner when she told me. She said her husband was so mad he used a whip."

"A belt."

"I'd do worse than that to Mary Surrey."

As I say, you can't tell one mother from the other. Karol and Nancy are as alike as two snails pulling into their shells.

I settle in the stillness of my room, which is as quiet as if beside a stream beneath a row of willows. As casually as setting myself on a smooth stone and unpacking

a picnic lunch by untying the knotted ends of a ging-
ham tablecloth, I spread out the years with Franklin
that I have carried wrapped so long.

In the coolness of my room, I see the iceberg of our
marriage surface. As through a windless sky of time,
I see old scenes with Franklin frozen in my mind.

See him, here. In times of drought we looked out in
the morning to dusty treetops, and, behind them, to
the burnt face of our hill. Franklin called this my waterhole, as if I were an eland coming here to drink
from the springs of solitude before going down to the
crowded day.

Here, at night, he watched me twist my long hair
round and round into a figure eight and pin it up. For
I was tidy then; it seemed to go with Franklin. With
Franklin I was not Egypt walking by the Nile; with
Franklin I was no one but myself.

For John I undid my hair as if I were again the native
girl I had played at on the beach, her skin scented with
oil, showing all she had. For him I climbed the steps to
rendezvous in a rented room that was for me a flowered
island daydream.

It was Franklin who shared with me the reality of
the actual ocean shore.

I see him, there.

On summer nights while I swam, with my suit off, against the current, he kept watch, hunting for tiny feeding crabs by flashlight, his pants' legs rolled carefully above his ankles, moving steady as a lighthouse up the beach, careful to step in open spaces bare of claws.

In the winter we wrapped ourselves in coats against chilling northers that brought with them wind-muffling fogs to blanket the night. In the dark, the land beneath our feet seemed to tilt with the undertow, as if it were about to slide into the sea. In the cold, we walked the ocean's rim. It became a ceremony to walk to the pier and back, with the flashlight scanning for shells. There was no need to talk; we found the act of walking itself communal.

Franklin was a man born on land who did not like to get his feet wet; he liked to keep the sea at a distance, to observe. I was a woman accustomed to the ocean, who liked to plunge in over her head in the submerged world of the great green anemones. There by the pier, at the water's edge, we were both at home.

As we waited to catch our frosty breaths we often quoted lines about the ocean. Cummings' was my favorite:

> *On such a night the sea through her blind*
> *miles*
> *Of crumbling silence seriously smiles*

The trip to the coast that Franklin enjoyed most was his present to me of the promised boat trip at Rockport to see the migratory birds. Although it was a way to return me to the sea, it allowed him to watch it, removed and dry, through field glasses.

Rockport is for fishermen. They come to lean all day on weathered piers, bleached and gray—the men, and the piers. The talk is of hurricanes: Fern, Beulah, Carla, Camille, those girls who ravage the islands, fill in the shallows, splinter the wooden houses that sway on stilts above the blowing grass. Here, birds from the north come in flocks to stand in the nearby marshes sharing the ocean's fish.

Crossing the plank onto our chartered boat I felt we were embarking on the fifth day of Creation: the channel waters were aswim with fish, the reeds gave refuge to wingéd birds. We traveled the lagoon, a backwater of that ancient ocean across the hillocks whose depths looked like a thousand thousand downpours of the Flood.

The Audubon ladies were in wrinkled denim and tennis shoes, peering through binoculars. Calling out the names of birds identified in Peterson's *Field Guide to Birds*—snowy egret, great blue heron, cormorant—they taught us to recognize a wide variety: dainty, white birds in golden slippers; spare, unmoving birds standing with one leg tucked up like a folded umbrella; gray-green birds with slanting wings, pink birds with flat spoonbills; gooselike swimming loons; long-legged waders. At last we saw, like pale apparitions, like vestiges from the time of Ahab, Jonah, Noah, the elongated white bodies of the rare whooping cranes. They were large, shy birds who did not intertwine their downy necks, did not touch one against the other. Each reticent bird, as if sensing us through the other end of a row of field glasses, stepped deliberately, slowly, backward in the marshy ground, retreating from our loud head count, "three . . . seven . . . eleven . . ."

We steamed like crabs in the sun on the long ride back, shading our eyes, squinting for another sign of white in the tall grasses. Franklin found some drinking water and studied his *Guide*, pleased with the task of identifying, while I talked to my new friend Velma.

Her tale of the four brothers who knocked on the door for breakfast was for me a glimpse of a more spontaneous family than I had known. Such surprises were not part of the style of either my family or Franklin's. Such a noisy family who played jokes on one another, who got together because they wanted to, who hugged and fought and touched and stormed, seemed to be what I was missing.

At the time the contrast made my own marriage seem as repetitious, as fixed, as the annual journey of birds to the coast. It was only later that I had empathy for Velma lying at daybreak in a husband's arms, with four Marshall brothers banging on the door.

Before we docked, one of the ladies told us a story that the others knew by heart, a dreadful violation of the sacred, by some man, whom they thought had been drunk, who last year had shot one of the protected cranes, and got off by paying a large fine. Listening, I stared at the curving back of the thirteenth crane, a quiet bird, standing half hidden in high grass, and tried to imagine a stain of red seeping through its white feathers, as if it were the victim of that hunter's bullet. The bird I watched, perhaps sensing the doom we discussed, threaded her way gingerly down to the water and began the slow downbeat of her enormous wings. Escaping before she became extinct . . .

As Velma said in a letter that came today: the grass is always greener.

When I left Franklin, it seemed to me a proper, clear decision. He and I were not good for each other; we reinforced in each other all that was lifeless and mannered. Although I had not known I was looking for a man like John, there he was, and he was what I needed. The strength to go through the bitterness, the property dispute, the custody arrangement—all the litigation that seemed at the time unclear, unkind, and that took far too long—came from the conviction that John was also what my son needed. I believed that in the long run it would be best for him to be around a different kind of father, a man like John, who would barge right in your door and put his arm around you and talk directly to you.

At least I talked myself into this position on my last visit to Franklin's mother's farm. Her acres of rich Blackland soil, which lie south of the North Fork River, are no longer used as a farm, except for a few cows that are kept down in the pasture and bred by the caretaker. Franklin's mother, Nonnie, calls it their Summer Place. But, except for fishing trips, in the summer it becomes too hot to stay there long. We used it —and they still do, apparently taking Babs along—as a weekend retreat, going up there with ice chests of drinks and picnic baskets of food.

At one time the men used it as a base to hunt from, and they still keep a hunting lease nearby, on some land north of the South Fork River. The house is new, as family homesteads go. Fifty years ago they had a large stone place, up the farm-to-market road, which was destroyed in a marathon downpour of thirty-six inches in less than twenty-four hours, a deluge said to be the greatest rainfall ever recorded, in that time, in U.S. history. They enjoy telling this good tale as it implies that their family goes back to the Flood.

Mostly, what I did on visits was to sit and rock with Nonnie, and listen to her soft Southern voice talk about her kin.

She was usually out of sorts with Franklin's sister, who was not behaving as a daughter should. "Little Nonnie, and her young man, her husband, I should learn to say by now, shouldn't I? After all, they've been married three years . . . Well, they have no use for this place and I wish they wouldn't feel they have to come on my account. It makes me as uncomfortable as it does them for them to be here. They're intractable. Does that mean stubborn? I hope so. Well, I mean they don't say a word they don't have to. They don't participate in anything. Why, Thanksgiving they wouldn't even walk down to the new tank to see the Angus bull."

It made her happier to talk of the days when Franklin's father was alive. "We used to have an old settee here." She would gesture to where we were sitting. "That got ruined by those hound dogs. But, after all, you can hardly ask a man to come out hunting without his dogs. He used to take all the men, and the dogs, and all the food my daughter and I could fix—she was helpful enough in those days—and," here she might wink at what she thought of as naughty boys, saying, "I wouldn't be surprised if they took a flask of whisky along, too, to keep themselves real warm." She would look toward the screen door of the house where Franklin was. "Ask that son of mine if he remembers hunting with his Dad. He'll remember."

When I was talked out, I would go down to watch the flock of Rambouillet sheep which someone kept across the river. Lying in clovered grass, I would watch the fat sheep move on cue in their slow and ruminating way. They would follow their leader, an old, matted ram. When he stood, the rest, lying puddled together, rose one by one to stand stolid in the rear like stuffed nursery lambs waiting for a sign to move on. By such unhurried maneuvers, they could work their way down to the lily-padded water for a drink, or trudge uphill to chew on taller grass. I liked best the rare occasions when the leader rose and waited for a good space of time and no one lifted a drowsy face to see, so that, overruled, he had to grudgingly reverse himself and lie back down.

On that last visit Nonnie and I were on the wide-plank porch fanning ourselves against the heat, and talking, while Franklin was doing some grouting work in the kitchen. He liked to keep things in good repair for his mother.

Nonnie said, "Ellen, honey, tell Franklin I wouldn't mind if he brought out some chairs and sat awhile; the sun's going down and we can watch the fireflies come out, and this swing is getting tiresome."

This message I dutifully gave to my husband, who sent word back, "Tell Mother there'll be mosquitoes out there on the porch; it's too calm to sit out this time of year."

To which she sent back, "Well, tell him to come on out while there's still a little daylight, before we have to start the supper."

Franklin patiently relayed that the sink still had a few more loose tiles he had to finish cementing. "Tell Mother I'll be there in a minute. It won't take much longer."

As I stood on the porch in the twilight, straining my eyes to see the woolly sheep lie down again, Frank came up the creaking wood steps from the meadow where he had been putting food out for the deer.

At six he had acquired that growing lack of confidence that comes from exposure to the public schools. He had begun the habit of glancing around at everyone before he did anything, as if to get the teacher's approval. It bothered me to see him have to check with adults before deciding what he thought; I had been more comfortable with him the year before, when he acted as if he owned most of the territory he knew.

He had started saying, "Please" and "May I?" and washing his hands before meals. I wish the schools did not think little boys have to be made so soon into gentlemen like their fathers.

In his overalls he looked like a boy who might play

a long-legged Jack and the Beanstalk: dutiful enough to bring the golden egg back to his mother, fearless enough to climb the strange vine after it.

Coming up between me and his grandmother, checking with both of us, he said, "Mom, ask Dad can we ride down in the jeep to see the cows before supper. Ask him can we, Mom."

He waited for me to take this message to the man who worked one room away.

Just as my daddy said, "Give the flowers to your mother," and Franklin said, "Tell Mother there will be mosquitoes on the porch," so Frank, like an observant schoolboy, was copying the grown-up men he knew.

"Tell him yourself, Frank," I said, no longer wanting to play the game. "He's in the house and he's got ears."

"Gee—"

It didn't matter that later we had generous ham sandwiches and cold Lone Star beer for supper, and stayed up to talk and watch clouds from the north promise rain and then blow over; except for the formalities, I had already left Frank's father on the front porch of Nonnie's Summer Place.

There were better things I could have done. There were ways I could have broken habits without breaking a marriage. If I had seen that then, there would have been more private places than a donut shop to hear the voice of Franklin say, "You're wearing your hair down."

But with John already there and waiting, every irritation became magnified. Love is a distorting glass we look through.

As Velma put it clearly in her letter:

> Dear Ellen,
> You must have heard it all by now. Can you imagine me, of all people, making a scandal in the church? If you want the truth, Oscar reminded me the first time he showed up of your previous husband who I met that time on the boat, who had Eyes for Nobody But You. But there you are with Johnny, having the brothers up to visit, going the Last Mile. As they say, the grass is always greener.
> I guess I'll be busy with these five of mine, and then Oscar has four himself, older, thank the Lord. If you feel like it you might write me some time at this address. It was good to know you, you were always good to me, and I hope we will keep in touch.
>
> Your friend,
Velma

The day repeats its pattern: there are children to get settled before the husband's homecoming. There is red to wear for going out in the married time of day.

. . .

Ellen Nor, bathed and fed, has her story. I tell Little Red Riding Hood, embellishing, making the wolf a proper villain. Making him a vain old fool admiring himself in Grandmother's cap and gown before an antique wardrobe mirror. Red, that silly girl, has eaten most of the donuts from her basket, the chocolate ones, leaving only a stale custard cream or two for Granny. She dawdles picking daisies. And why not? Grandmother bores, talks about the good old days: if only we had not sold the farm back when we did. It is no disappointment to Red when she finds that black bewhiskered face peering out of the four-poster bed. Ellen Nor acts out the great escape and falls into the saving arms of the woodsman—the elephant, of course.

Frank is home from eating pizza with his friends. He finds me on the stairs and asks, "Do I have to change my shirt?" His tone says he doesn't want to.

He still has on the blood-stained T-shirt from school. Dried, the spots could easily be mistaken for mud, but I don't tell him that.

"You can leave it on to show John."

"I guess I'll have to tell him about it."

"I called him—"

He tries to read my face. "Yeah, that's good. I didn't get time to."

When I am upstairs I hear from below the loud electric sounds of the record I am not allowed to play. He must have put it on to give him confidence before John comes home. It is pleasant dressing to the wailing sounds of organ music that remind me of a fifteenth-century mass.

While I shower I try to think of how to tell John about seeing Franklin. But each time I get the setting, the dark table in the Greek restaurant where not even the waiters know our names, I cannot find the words. To say to him, "Franklin bought me a donut," is not to tell him what happened. To say how moved I was to stand at the corner stopped by a red light and see my former husband and hear him say my name, is to tell too much. There does not seem to be a way to describe perceiving again the constancy of Franklin's person, his dependability, his air that he will be the same tomorrow as he is today, without suggesting that I wish I were with him still.

John and I used to talk about Franklin, but it was in the worried tones that the brothers use for Harold: poor Harold. John wanted then to be kind to Franklin, as is his way, but it was not suitable to me in a situation where kindness was the final added insult.

At least I won't bring that pity back; I can do that much for Franklin. Rather than say that he looked thin and slightly stooped, I will tell John that my old husband has at last a steady girl, and she is really pretty.

. . .

When Franklin agreed to the divorce, he said, "You're making a mistake."

"Then I'll pay the price."

This afternoon he must have felt like a banker, collecting, when I drank his cup of coffee.

I dress for an evening out with John in long pants and a narrowed halter top of scarlet silk. My hair is brushed loose and full. Around my neck I hang gold chains and put gold loops at my ears. I darken my eyelids with kohl, redden my lips with gloss, and put the dusty purple scent of heliotrope behind my ears and at my wrists.

I didn't dress like this for Franklin. The one time I went out in a plunging neckline above an empire waist that was the fashion, he complained, "Leave that kind of dress for the ones who are advertising. It makes me think you are still looking around."

"How do you want me to look, then?"

"I like it when you look content," he said.

Did his sharp eyes see discontent today?

Downstairs I call for John.

I find him in the living room listening to Frank's still outraged account of White Hog and the boys.

They are not alone.

"Come on in." John gets up and comes to me. "You look great," he says. Then, hesitant, he gestures to the couch. "I prevailed on Pete here to come by and give us some medical advice on Frank's nose. On the phone I couldn't tell; I thought it might be broken."

He has not played fair with me, asking company in. Pete's being here makes me feel an overdressed wife.

Frank says importantly, "They don't think the cartilage is hurt." He even offers to let me touch his nose.

What I thought was to be a private time has once again become a crowd. John collects people; he cannot help himself.

"Evening, Ellen." Pete rises too and bestows a damp kiss on me. "You sure are kind to let me drop in like this." He tries to sound professional. "I don't think your boy is too bad off." He is palpating Frank's nose to earn his Scotch and soda. But direct contact with injury gives him a fit of sneezing.

"Bless you," I say. Please go home.

John pulls me close, his hand finding and lingering on my bare back. "I was just getting ready to tell them a story." He puts his other arm across Frank's shoulder; he likes to have all his audience close at hand. "You didn't know my brother, Fred, did you, Frank? He was the best of the lot; but he was also the runt of the litter, always getting himself into trouble. One day he got in a fight like yours at school. Same thing exactly:

three boys ganged up on him and fairly well beat him up. He got his on the rock pile behind the school. The next day he really got even: he put garbage in their desks, which really smelled things up, and the teacher made them clean it out and sent them to detention hall."

"What did they do to Uncle Fred for that?" Amazement is written on my twelve-year-old's face.

"They beat him up again, what else?" John and Pete have a good laugh.

Frank seems proud to have reminded John of a story. Maybe he can see himself become a family legend as the first Marshall ever to get jumped by blacks at school. He stands a minute more under John's arm. But then it is obvious he finds it too awkward. After all, he wasn't born into that clan; it isn't really his uncle whom John tells about.

"We didn't get dessert at Brewster's house?" He makes this a question in my direction.

"Look in the kitchen." I give him a chance to leave. "There may be butterscotch pie." Nancy sometimes does the recipe on a box of pudding mix when she comes to babysit.

Pete lights a cigar, which makes him smell like my grandfather. He wipes his watery eyes and turns to John with talk of golf stories about his father, who plays the Senior Circuit. His anecdotes spin out like a spider's web for two long drinks that use up the minutes of my evening. His smoke creates a setting that makes wives out of place; I should be rocking in the corner, attending to a lap of needlepoint.

His glass empty, Pete says to me, "John tells me you're on your way out to eat." Hopeful.

"He tells me that, too."

"Hope it's all right if I tag along. My bachelor cooking sure leaves something to be desired." He wipes his eyes and waits.

John is waiting too.

"Do come, Pete. We always like to have company."

John looks at me gratefully. He is glad to have his balding lonesome friend included. It bothers him to see a man of nearly forty with no woman at home to fix supper for him.

Pleased to be welcome, Pete wipes his big golf-burned face with his wrinkled blue handkerchief and redoubles his efforts to be entertaining. I make a shallow attempt to respond to the talk while John moves back and forth between us, wanting the people he likes to like each other.

I haven't learned to live with what I thought I wanted: everyone is always *we* to John.

When we are finally in the car headed for supper no one talks about where we'll go. It is assumed we will eat at the club, which is not at all the setting I had planned.

We get settled at the bar, which is full of couples whom we know and wave to. The waiter, who knows our names, sets bowls of peanuts and popcorn on our table and takes our customary order.

When John and I were meeting secretly in the mornings he used to talk of bringing me here. "I want to walk right in that door with you beside me, and have Toby say, 'Evening, Mr. Marshall,' and have all our friends look up and say, 'There's John and Ellen,' just like we belonged together." Now here we are as we have been so many times before—waiting in this dark room to have Toby bring us our usual drinks while Pete blows his nose. To be here cannot be the reason we broke up a marriage and betrayed a man.

Our friends at the tables around us resemble us: they are too dressed up, and they are getting drunk. With each new round someone breaks out in a loud laugh over a commonplace comment. Like us, they are noisy on the surface to drown out the undercurrents between them. I tell John, "I'll have another Scotch."

"I thought we'd eat." John treads on the obvious, that I have had too much.

"Just the three of us?" I look around, sure a party will appear.

As if on cue, one rushes in, stage right.

"Ellen!" It is Karol's voice, shrieking from the entrance to the bar. With her, bearing down on us, comes a man of unsavory character.

"Heaven help us," Pete, her some-time date, murmurs. "She sure can pick the losers." He excepts himself, of course.

"This is Nookie, everybody," Karol presents him.

"John Marshall," says John, getting up, shaking hands, pulling out their leather chairs. "Pete, I think you know—" He looks at me. "We were getting ready to go in to eat."

There hangs a moment, suspended like a swing at the top of its climb, in which I could rescue us, could adjourn with Pete and John to hear them finish up winning shots from the sand trap, the June primary runoff, and the stolen Kawasaki.

But I do not rise to the occasion. "Eat with us," I urge them. "John is looking for company tonight." Why not give him what he wants: a fun time around the dinner table. We'll all have lots of wine, tell funny stories, and come rolling in, John and his wife, at two o'clock, dropping our shoes in the hall, our clothes on the stairs. We'll say, "That dreadful man, you could have oiled the Queen Mary with him," and then fall together into sex, screwing like strangers, like married people.

"Karol," I say to get the ball rolling when they have accepted and settled themselves over drinks, "you've got a new dress."

Her strident voice answers on cue. "I should hope to God. It's my turn and then some. After those girls get through with their hot pants and their long pants and their Hang-Tens and their Charlie's Girls, I'm usually wearing flour sacks."

Nookie oils out a compliment about the dress, which he feels with practiced fingers.

He goes on pawing her even as we unroll our napkins and pull up our chairs. "I told Karol I wouldn't stand for that long-haired boy hanging around her eldest like a dog in heat. I have some standards." He checks to be sure we hear that he is claiming ownership.

John and Pete appear to have turned to stone. In silence they study the menus.

"My God," Karol turns on Pete, "you've got a sunburn. You didn't get that doing prostates."

Pete twitches like a rabbit. "Sure like your dress, Karol."

Nookie leans toward me, ingratiating. "*You* can't be the mother of that young man I saw in front of your house tonight."

"You may be right," I say.

Everybody laughs uproariously.

John looks up. In the sudden silence as we catch our breath to begin again, he meets my eyes. He looks hurt and perplexed. But I turn away. He wanted company this evening; so I've arranged to have some. Let there be cake, invite all the peasants in, she said, in her backless ruby red . . . I pick up my menu; my steak is long overdue.

Karol and I have a lot to talk about while the men order wine: her girls, her invalid mother, my son's mangled face, the crappy things that happened at the agency this afternoon. "You wouldn't believe," she tells me, "how crappy people are."

"I didn't think you'd mind Pete," John says, when we are upstairs in my room at last.

"You said no goings or comings."

"But this morning we didn't know about Frank."

"You said."

"When I heard he'd got ganged up on I wasn't even sure you'd still want to go out. That was a real shock, and after that boy drowned, too."

"I did."

"You can't be that inflexible. You have to be willing to shift your plans when something like that comes up."

"Anything is an excuse for you to include somebody else."

"It wasn't me who invited that Nookie to dinner."

"I thought any crowd would do."

John is displeased with me—because I was drunk and disorderly and brought Karol and her creep home for a nightcap, which Pete, getting hives, begged off from. Nookie said we ought to get a player piano for the sunporch. I guess they're next door now rolling in the hay, whispering so as not to wake Mother and the girls.

John strains to get through to me. He is unhappy that I have misunderstood his good intentions. "But it matters a lot who the people are. Don't you see? That's the point. There is a limit to the hours in the day; it's hard to make the time you want for the people that you love." He goes on, dogged, in the face of my silence. "When Fred died—" his voice breaks, "when Fred died it made us all realize how quick time goes. As Harold said then, 'It's already afternoon and the day is growing shorter all the time.'"

"Fourscore and ten." I am familiar with Harold's way of keeping time.

John takes offense at my tone. "What does that mean?"

"It means that preachers get help from the Bible to keep track of things."

"Are you making fun of Harold?"

"No, no, truly, John." Even tonight I know that this brother is sacrosanct.

"Well, I never know when you are kidding."

"I'm not. Never. I'm never kidding."

He does not understand; my being serious is different from his being serious. He undresses to his shorts, throwing things around, his shirt on the floor, his trousers on the bed, one shoe is lying on its side in the middle of the floor. My room looks like a rummage sale.

He is pacing, as he does when things need talking out. He thinks with his body. In turn he rotates his arms, limbers up his shoulders, and touches his toes. He practices somatic medicine.

He pursues his point. "Last week you were put out when I brought your own brother home to dinner."

"Edward and I do all right."

"You ought to be proud of him."

"Why? Because he is annihilating his wife?"

"His being a doctor and all, good enough to interview at the clinic."

"I grew up on my-father-the-doctor. That takes away all the mystique."

"You could encourage him—"

"He doesn't need it. He knows that within the limited frontiers of the A.M.A. he'll do all right."

"That's condescending." John sounds as offended as though I were running down his own schooling. He says, "My mother gave me a lot of support through law school. She didn't have much else to give, but she gave us all that."

"I'm not his mother."

"You're his family, just the same."

"He can make it by himself. He and Laura Ann both can. I did her more harm than good nagging her for a

breakfast egg. That was your idea, that I intrude up
there in the midst of her bad time."

"I bet you helped," he insists. "Sometimes all a person needs is just to talk it out. You said she broke down
and told you a lot of things. When Harold did that,
we all thought it helped him."

Harold again. "Poor Velma—speaking of being
ganged up on by three boys in your advisory. You all
took care of her."

John withdraws at criticism of his brothers. "She
didn't even leave his clothes clean or the dishes washed.
And it was Saturday night, the night before church,
and he was working on his sermon."

Imagine, Velma: not only adultery, but bad maid
service. The mind grows faint. "I can't remember, did
I take Franklin's shirts to be ironed before I left? Can
you remember if I took his gray suits to be pressed?"
I lean my shoulder against the wall for balance as I
slip off my sandaled heels.

John is the wrong person to be sarcastic to. It makes
him get out his defenses, makes him burrow in. It was
not used at his house. The Marshall boys were brought
along with other prods. The gist of which was that
they had one another. After all, if there were five of
you, you had to believe that making it together was

the only way. And if you were their mother, trying to feed and clothe them all and get them through college, you had to convey the air that this crowd, this excess of kin, was the point, the heart of the matter. Which she did faithfully until she died and went to her reward —the nature of which I will leave to Harold, that authority.

John especially believes in his family, as he grew up surrounded by them: two older to look up to, and two younger to set an example for. He also grew up with the conviction that if you do your best you get rewarded for it.

All his life for his hard work and good intentions he has received: paste-on lambs at Sunday School, Boy Scout badges, debating medals, elected campus offices, the choice jobs, and even, in the end, the girl. A man used to such awards finds it hard to be punished for such well-meaning gestures as bringing my brother home for supper or bringing Pete by to look at his stepson's battered face. He wants us all to see that he always goes out of his way for any member of either of our families.

He does not understand that what he considers my lack of loyalty to my brother and son is rather that they are such a part of me that I assume they can walk on their feet of clay and don't need special treatment.

What John needs is a wife who will follow the Boy

Scout creed, and be all those things I haven't been: loyal, trustworthy, obedient, thoughtful, all the rest. Surely friendly is the first.

But the fault is mine for taking the job if I never intended to give out merit badges. He didn't hide his need for trophies. He spelled it out in a dozen ways: "A man like that deserves some reward for sticking to his job," "When I was on campus we tried to single out the guys who deserved it and give them a little recognition," "All the plaques they hand out at those service groups downtown don't mean what they ought to; some fellows have worked a lot harder than others," "Mother had us trained; I guess she had to when she was gone all day. Even as little kids we got a red star for stuff we were supposed to do all the time, like make our bunks, and a gold one for extra jobs," "Ellen, it isn't my business, at least not yet, but it doesn't sound to me like Franklin ever gives your boy enough credit for what he does."

John chins himself now in the doorway, while he works out the words to make it clear to me that he meant well this evening, and that I have misunderstood. He will forgive me my bad manners because he wants us to get along. He chins himself, but he thinks of how to come to me.

I take off the gold at my ears and around my neck

and jiggle it to hear it clank together like small copper bells. When Franklin lived here we did not chin ourselves to stay in shape; we shaped ourselves by ceremony. Sometimes, if we had stayed up late like tonight, we toasted the evening with hot chocolate, drunk from cups saved for special occasions—old English cups as veined as my mother's hands, which had been bought for her in New Orleans by her father. The cups were as lovely as a pair of delft blue tulips in the greenness of my room . . .

John stops his exercise to ask, "Are you going to stand there like that all night?"

"I used to drink hot chocolate in this room."

He stiffens, the bulk of him draws back. "Sorry, that was before my turn."

Which brings it up at last. "I saw Franklin today."

"Did you?"

"After I was down to sign the papers on the farm. He bought me a cup of coffee and donuts for Ellen Nor."

A muscle jumps in his jaw. "What did he want?"

I wish I knew; not me, I think. "He has a girl."

"It's taken him long enough." He lets me know how fast, he, John, would hit the ground rutting if the shoe were switched.

"He's getting thin."

"He always was. Frail, if you ask me." He scowls. "Frank said his dad told him he could change schools.

I told him he had to stick it out. There've been fights in schools since the one-room schoolhouse. Franklin hasn't any right to move that boy around; he acts like he owns him."

Today, Franklin acted the same with me. I shrug, not wanting to arbitrate between two fathers. "That's Frank's decision."

"The boy's too young to decide a thing like that himself."

"Ask your brothers, then," I snap. "Set up a committee to decide. Fly down there. Fly them up here."

I have gone too far. He stands still looking at me, his face turning a dark red. "While we're on the subject of your coming downtown today, Ellen, I can tell you that you sure upset Peggy."

"*Peggy?*"

"She says you look down on her. And I guess you do." He lets me know that he and his secretary had to talk about the wife's attitude, that he had to give his Peggy reassurance, maybe slip his arm around her waist while she made some mascaraed tears.

It is the last straw, which John cannot see—that their talking of me together is the final invasion of our privacy. I strike at him as hostile as the boys at school. "I did look down on her; she was sitting, I was standing."

The muscle jumps.

I see that he is jealous; that he has told me his story

of the office in an attempt to retaliate for my seeing Franklin. But that is not fair: he beat Franklin out in the first race. Men, however, confuse love with competition always. Now he continues to compete with Franklin for the authority over, the jurisdiction over, their son.

A second time this evening I let a moment hang, then let it pass the wrong way. There is a moment during which we stand glaring, angry, when I could reach out to him the easy way. I have only to drop my halter to the floor and cross the space between us, to lean my red silk legs against him and offer him his reward at last.

Instead I continue to lean against the wall, quiet as the ruffled ferns growing by the window.

Having nothing more to say, John roots around on his closet floor for his corduroy bathrobe. Into my silence he asks stiffly, "You won't mind if I work awhile downstairs? I need to finish up this brief so she can get it typed by noon."

"—I may go on to sleep; I've had too much to drink."

"Goodnight, then."

Alone, I grow disorderly. I drop my things one by one across the celery rug: halter, slacks, hose, panties, jangling earrings, chains, and bangles. Earlier I behaved as a shrew; now I act the part of slattern.

Such behavior is a symptom easy to diagnose: I'm wanting what I had and lost. Hot chocolate, in part.

T H R E E

Friday, June 2

A fog came in with daybreak. Over breakfast we looked into a mist so dense we could not see past the largest oak tree. Now, the haze burned off by the sun, the day is as light and dry as the clearest wine. Gardening under this cloudless blue enameled sky, I find the air fresh to breathe. Before Ellen Nor comes out, I work the ground; kneeling in the cloying, clinging fragrance of gardenia, I loosen the dry ground around the roses.

My birthday plans have changed. There is a party scheduled here for all my kin, and John's. There is even a cake baking in Nancy's mother's oven.

Although it will be a change for me—growing older inland from the water's edge—my absence will not make a difference to the coast. As before, the ocean will beat against the heavy sand shelf making salt spray fly into the air under the white bellies of seagulls. Again, the tide will slide, ebbing, out to sea, to rage continents away, crashing on foreign shores, to swell back bringing scraps of rubber trees and coconuts.

What I remember of Galveston will stay the same.

By the water is the sea wall; down the beach stand motels on piers; the ship channel is bevied with shrimpers returning home; seaweed washes in with surfers, and babies sunburn under towels draped over open car windows.

The town that butts against the ever-present waves has streets with names as familiar to me as my own, and more pleasing. Its old Victorian showplaces, built to buttress their inhabitants from commerce, house old families who do not speak to new families. In the outskirts live new families who do not speak to transient families. Apart from these is the medical school, which is an island on an island.

Walking to the beach from Mother's house I would again pass leaning rental houses covered with vines that climb rapidly in the humid air. The fog, that only visits us here, lives on the cobbled streets at home, going out and coming in on schedule like a streetcar. At the shore, with the salt clinging to your skin and tasting on your lips, the heavy air breeds lungs that find this inland air dry and difficult to breathe.

At Mother's house we live at the back, in the kitchen and on the porch. The kitchen is where John, the favorite house guest, sits at the table while the cornbread bakes; the screened porch is where Mother keeps her garden tools, her clay pots, and, in wooden trays, those plants ready to be set out. It is at the back of the house,

on the back steps, where Mother and I sit looking out
toward the yard together, talking of her flowers.

The front of Mother's house is a parlor, hung with
curtains heavy with dust; it is a place to entertain
strangers, a ghost of a room, its antiques the shades of
generations past.

Upstairs is her bed. It is *her* bed because she was born
in it, has shared it for thirty-seven years with my
father, and will doubtless die in it. It is no wonder that
such a woman, who will have spent her nights in one
four-poster bed of massive oak, found my rebedding
and remarriage difficult to accept.

Here, away from the sea, dry days are back and the
ground is as baked as if the rains had never come. We
keep sprinklers going at dawn and dusk to keep our
green alive. In the hard ground I work with gloves and
trowel.

Ellen Nor says, "We can go swing for your birthday."

She is tanned as brown as peanut butter. She has on
a playsuit she got herself into and keds that aren't tied.
Her independence does not include brushing her hair.

"Let's go to the playground, then, and swing."

She has a piece of breakfast bacon in her hand. Casually upsetting my customary schedule she calls, "Bad dogs—," and Fang and Wolf come bounding into my yard in the wrong time of day. They take my daughter's food and lick her fingers gratefully, and, in parting, stop to fertilize a bed of sweet alyssum. This is her present to me.

We like the nearby sunken grassy playground, which was once a quarry. Ellen Nor likes it now, for it is busy with summer children out of school who swing and ride the small merry-go-round. I like it because it once was a swimming pool for marine lizards of great size. I always think when we come that we may happen upon the gaping jaw or recurved teeth of a mosasaurid, lying exposed in the lowest field, where boys today have made a baseball diamond.

We have a busy morning: we throw two sticks for transient beagles, we return one tennis ball where it has rolled from higher ground, we step in one pile left by a cat and have to take our shoes off, we watch one boy climb a tall rope ladder and fall off. While Ellen Nor fights with a bigger girl over a vacant swing and wins, I find and pocket seven small cephalopods, each curved like a ram's horn at the end. I am the seventh daughter of the seventh daughter who has combed the seven seas for seven shells.

Tired, we sit down and spread out our legs on a grassy ledge halfway up the quarry's rim. In the shade of a stunted mesquite growing out of a crack in the rocks, our seats give us a good view of the ballgame down below.

At Ellen Nor's feet we find a used condom.

"Mama, look—a balloon?" She is not sure.

"I don't think that's what it is."

"The balloons at my birthday were red." She throws it down the hill.

"—It may be part of a rubber glove like the ones Nancy uses to clean the oven." Which is a dishonest remark and I do not like myself for making it. When she is grown she will remember that I lied. Girls remember.

It sounds like the sort of evasion my mother handed me; it must go with the role of being a mother. She was given to saying, "You'll have time enough to go into all that when you get married," or "You'll find out all about that when you're married." Such comments to girls make marriage seem the answer to all secrets. No wonder we rush into it.

Next time we find an adult clue lying on the ground, I must have courage enough to say, "That's for boys to use when you are living with them. The way you'll do, maybe, in Paris and in London and on a summer trip to Africa, if you feel like it."

When she is that age she'll appreciate that I told her the truth, and, barefoot, she'll strut in the door for my fiftieth birthday, with a canvas knapsack on her back, to surprise me with a backbone of some special note. It won't be her best find, of course, but perhaps her second best.

"Grown-up girls," I say, to make amends, "when they leave home, can sometimes sleep out in the park."

"They might get hungry and go home." She qualifies such freedom.

Which makes it time, as our stomachs count, for tuna salad and iced tea with lime on linen mats at home.

By afternoon, Nancy, who has switched her days so she can help me, and I have given the house a company look. The brick floors have been scrubbed, the wood chests and tables have been waxed to a glow, and the reds and golds in our faded rugs seem brighter. We have set extra tables, with woven Mexican mats, out on the sunporch. Fourteen crystal wine glasses catch sunlight coming through the curtains and bounce miniature rainbows onto the amber flocked wallpaper. From the kitchen comes the smell of smoked turkey and baked ham and a casserole of cheese and grits and jalapeños. We have been busy.

She calls me in to see the lacy beige birthday cake that has just been delivered.

"It's beautiful, Nancy."

"My mother bake it."

It has toasted almonds on top of three tiers iced in a pale almond color. "What kind is it?"

"She only make spice cake with seafoam."

"My mother makes fresh coconut cakes . . ."

"She coming?"

"Yes. All of them—my brother, John's brothers. Karol. And the doctor."

"That man comin' with her?"

"He's supposed to."

She sticks out her tongue for the likes of Nookie. She never has much patience with Karol's choices. In part that's because Nancy has lived with one man for twenty years, though she's my age exactly.

"That girl comin'?"

"Who?"

"Who loss the baby."

"Yes. Laura Ann."

"She is sure the prettiest thing."

"She is."

Nancy sighs. "My sister have loss four herself." She transfers the cake to a cut-glass platter of my grandmother's and sets it carefully on top of the refrigerator out of reach of children's fingers.

All my party needs is flowers, and I do them now. I bring in most of what is in bloom outside and pile them on the counter. I mass small bouquets of early summer's fiery colors—the vivid oranges of cosmos and marigolds, the reds of portulaca and calendula—to set on the dining table, which is dressed with a bright woven cloth and brass trays and candle holders. In two large straw baskets stand jars of tangerine tiger lilies and white iris to go on each side of the fireplace. The shasta daisies make crowded nosegays for the sunporch tables. This work takes garden color to every room downstairs and leaves a mess of leaves and stems and shedding blooms littering the kitchen floor.

I leave these for Nancy. "Do I need to get anything while I'm out?" She keeps track.

"Your mother drink Sanka."

"She does; I forgot. I'll tell her you remembered."

"She likes biscuits."

"Biscuits?"

"You get me some Bisquick and I'll make some for you."

"What else?"

"You got enough candles?"

Candles. Birthdays must have candles. Not only tapers on the table but a dozen yellow votive candles in small glass circles to set around. "I'll get some more. And crackers for the cheese ball Karol is bringing over."

Nancy is unimpressed. "I saw her make it yesterday; it didn't look like much to me."

"We don't any of us cook like our mothers, Nancy. Our daughters will have to do better."

"I doubt those girls of hers will be cooking at all. And that baby of yours will be just like that wildcat of mine; she don't eat anything but Cokes."

"Things may change by then."

Nancy nods her head. "They will change by then for sure."

We all change, not suddenly, but gradually. Just as this week my visit to John's office to tell his Peggy goodbye made a small change between us, just as, later, my calling Franklin on the phone made a change between him and his twelve-year-old. The birthday coming inland is but an outward notice of these private alterations.

On my way to the store I drive down by the river, making a smaller birthday pilgrimage. A few sailboats —sunfish and dolphins—go under the bridge. On a familiar side street I park the car in front of an apartment building. Six years ago it was badly in need of paint; now it has been stuccoed over and the new façade painted used-car gold. Plastic geraniums sit in styrofoam pots in the flowerbeds where our old landlady once grew pink peonies and lavender hydrangeas. A sign directs applicants to apartment 504, where the manager handles rentals; beneath it another sign prohibits children and dogs.

The room that John and I rented has its blinds down. It is the sort of room in which you can imagine a divorcing couple, arguing while they carry coffee cups around and empty clothes from the closet and take down pictures that leave nail holes in the peeling walls, and throw their few valuable belongings on that lumpy bed as they shout their accusations to the papered wall. Someone is there now in that room I no longer have a key to open.

The first time I came I had waited a minute in the car to catch my breath, under old shade trees that hung down almost to touch the tops of garbage cans across the street. Then it was a street so old it already had cracked sidewalks too rough for rollerskating, almost too broken for walking children. It was already zoned for filling stations and drive-in groceries as well as apartment dwellers.

Before John came I walked up the stairs, through a maze of musty hallways, to the door that had our number on it. Once inside the room I sank in terror on that bed, that creaky bed, and stared at the lavish faded cabbage roses.

In the movies girls always wait for lovers in their slips; I had no slip. To show that I was staying I took off my shoes and undid my pinned-up length of hair. I can still feel the sag of that bed, see the landlady-pinks and violets of that room with its chenille spread, its old chintz chair, its threadbare flowered rug. It did not seem a room where anyone would come to see you unless he also had a key.

After we were lovers, after we had lain many times on the sheets and made the small talk about "when were you sure" and "what will we do now" that goes with such a bed, John said, "It took me awhile to get you here."

"I was scared."

"Of me?"

"—of putting myself on your pillow."

"Are you glad you did?" John even then liked to be told the obvious.

"You know I am, love. You found what I have kept out of reach all my life."

"Of Franklin?" Delighted to have bested the unsuspecting Hawkins.

"Of everyone."

"Not of me."

"No, not you. Never you."

"We can't keep this up for long; I hate this sneaking around. You'll have to tell him."

"How can I? Give me a little time—"

And again he had. He waited, locking and unlocking our borrowed door, through the spring as he had waited all the Christmas season to get me into that room.

He came to parties alone and left alone, a hard thing for a man like John. He brought me drinks and talked to Franklin and our friends. He heard and told and laughed at the same stories many, many times over:

"The only amateur I ever saw at work was this girl who followed the basketball team—"

"They're a lower rent crowd than you're used to."

"We had one solid sky full of birds in our sights, let me tell you—"

With mornings in a rented room as promise, he waited until after my trip to Nonnie's place.

And then he had to hear it at a garden cocktail party full of bouffant hair, sleeveless dresses, and masses of yellow florist's flowers. Off to ourselves, away from where the three-piece band was playing, beside a row of hurricane lanterns, he leaned down to be sure he heard. "Are you saying you will leave him?"

"Yes, I'm ready." My voice was almost a whisper. "Don't you see I'm wearing red?" I had kept an old promise in a cherry polka-dotted cotton.

"I forgot." He laughed because he was elated. "I wish I could announce it in the middle of the table."

"It won't be too long."

"Then I guess we shouldn't meet again?" He knew that; he was the lawyer.

"That's why I told you here—" And with all the crowd around us hugging and talking I gave him back the key.

. . .

I get back in the car. There is no use staring at plastic plants and a room with its shades down; there is Bisquick to buy and Sanka. There is not time to stand here on this rundown shady street like a schoolgirl holding to a memory. When I drive back across the bridge the sailboats have all gone miles downstream like papers scattering in the wind. I can make out one white sail against the shore.

Last Monday I went downtown to finish up the papers on the farm. Trained by my mother to give farewell gifts and mind my manners, I took a box of Godiva chocolates to this Peggy whom John had said was leaving. After managing the elevator without my daughter, I went back through the Looking Glass to where I was the boss' wife.

Peggy was animated when I came in. "He's busy just now." She laid out carbon paper for a very important brief.

"John said you were leaving?" I offered her the box of candy tied with a gold cord string.

"I guess you're glad of that." She flushed, but met my eyes.

"Why should I be glad?" But it had not been necessary to ask. I could see it on her face.

"I guess it's no secret how I feel."

"I didn't know." Which was the foolish truth.

"He did. He knew it all along." She looked at John's door, her chin up, love on her face. She implied that John had known a lot he hadn't told me.

I hesitated. My chocolates looked like thirty pieces of silver. There didn't seem to be much to say. "John said you were looking for another job."

This got her back up. "There's a lot of jobs I can get. I won't have any trouble getting a job." She informed me of this with pride. "I may move to a bigger place, you know, like Houston, or even Dallas. There are lots of lawyers in Dallas. I don't have to stay put in one town all my life."

"I'm sure you could."

"Besides, there's nothing to hold me here in this town any more."

"No," I said, "there isn't." The silence between us grew awkward.

"I may go someplace else," she repeated, not looking at me.

When John came out his secretary was typing eighty words a minute; his wife was standing with a box of chocolates in her hand.

He was nervous. "I told you I was losing Peggy?" He spoke to me but he looked anxiously at her.

"Yes. We have been talking about the opportunities in bigger cities." I tried not to be looking down on anyone when I said that.

She was all business. "I put the deeds by the file cabinet, Mr. Marshall."

"Thank you, Peggy." He took me into his office.

On my way out, after my name was witnessed, and we had made married talk about the children and our plans for the evening, I stopped at her desk to say goodbye.

"Now don't rush off," she said to me in front of John.

"Frank is due home from school," I said, to sound domestic.

John, relieved, led the next client in, slapping him on the back.

Alone, I told her, "I'm sorry," and I meant it.

"Goodbye, Mrs. Marshall." She was not red-eyed, and her back was straight; this was still her territory for another week.

With no one to help me cross the street, and no one to offer me coffee at a counter, it was difficult to navigate downtown in the afternoon.

That girl with her heart on her pants suit sleeve showed me what a warm existence she could create if she were married to a man like John. She made clear that a man like John—a Student Body President whose silver spurs still serve as bookends in his office—deserved better than he got at home.

The fault was mine: I had punished him for being what I most wanted. Married to Franklin, convinced that the confinement of our habits was imposed by him, not able to see that Franklin, accustomed to providing, must have constructed our routine to meet my needs, I had wanted John in my room. To inhabit it, to litter it, to undo my austere and scheduled existence. I had asked the Prince to ride up my glass mountain on his horse, and then withheld the golden oranges . . .

The fault was mine to think that if you have the overview the rest will fall in place. Although it is important to note the shells calcified in our hill, reminders that our turn will come to be imbedded too, and although it is the secret of time to know that when you walk on the past you walk on the present too, a woman should see that there are other ways to measure life. A Peggy would have known when to take a coffee break from geologic time.

A Peggy would have done it differently from the beginning . . .

John and I honeymooned in Mexico City. It was a city of crowds, of eight million people who seemed always to be moving: thousands walked four abreast down the sidewalk, thousands more rode honking by in old cars, flowing around the curving *glorietas* like a river of traffic. Surrounded by others we held hands and walked the length of the Reforma to see the golden lighted buildings of the Zócalo. We sat at twilight on a bench in the Romanesque square as the sky darkened like a forest and pigeons flew up into the naves of the cathedral as if into the highest branches to roost for the night.

There, in an aging, flowering, foreign world, I spent a week following a story of the sea. A story that was begun by those who crossed the water in boats of reeds, who left behind unexplained clues: Oriental cheekbones, Polynesian monoliths, Egyptian bulrushes. Continued in the mystery of Teotihuacán, whose dry-land pyramids were covered with ornate legendary sea serpents undulating over conch shells. These pyramids had, in turn, been buried by the gaudy conquering Aztecs, on whose bloody backs the Spaniards later erected the present spires of Catholic churches. This whole layered tomb of history—which began on a mat of grasses in a marsh that once had been a lake—was preserved by molten lava from the great twin volcanoes. It was an incredible glimpse for me of the many people who had come inland from the sea.

While I studied past cultures John moved happily from drinking salty margaritas and listening to the bands of strumming mariachis to eating roast *cabrito* under a waterfall of purple flowering bougainvillea.

At dawn on the waiting sheets of our hotel bed a Peggy would have said to him, "Love, you are my journey's end."

When our daughter was born a year later, John brought me scarlet ribbons for my hair, a crimson gown, and two dozen deep-red roses. All of his brothers came to see his child and pass around cigars.

"They gave me a hard time," he said, holding my hand in the bed. "For taking so long."

"They don't mind a girl?"

"Girls are still news to the Marshalls."

"Will you want to make another one?"

"Not unless you do. We have little Frank."

"A son of your own?"

"Possession is nine points of the law. If you raise a boy at your house that makes him your son." He seemed surprised. "I never think of Frank like that, as not being mine."

"I'm glad."

"Not that I don't wish sometimes that that frail banker hadn't got there before I did." He tried to say it lightly, but it was clear it was a thorn in his side not to have been the first with his own wife. "But," he made a story of it, "that's the story of my life, getting there late. Even the girl we all screwed in high school got knocked up by the captain of the football team."

"Did you wish you had beat him there?"

"Not and get slapped with having to marry her." He had looked pleased to remember his wilder self. He added, "She did have a nice strawberry mark."

"Do you wish I had?"

"Not and been laid by the football team."

"I wasn't."

"I know." He squeezed my hand. "It took me a year to get you away from that limp-wristed husband." He lit his cigar, not bothered by the no-smoking sign. "You ought to keep your hair loose like that all the time. I like it."

"What shall we name her?" My new responsibility was on my mind.

"I thought we'd call her after you."

"What about your mother?"

"Harold beat me to it. Remember he has little Hilda."

"Ellen, then." Instead of Jack as he had planned.

The thought of rearing a girl had seemed a heavy task to me when she was ten hours old. The path to womanhood is so strewn with the obstacles of Barbie dolls and bake-sets. Already the brothers had arrived with bouquets of pink gowns and pinafores. The night nurse had brought her to me with a pink bow in her hair. "A girl is hard to raise," I said.

A Peggy would have pulled him against the crimson

nylon gown and whispered, "Love, love, you could father an army."

Even last Monday night, when I offered John my birthday here, it was the kind of gesture I knew how to make; a Peggy would have known how to give him more.

John had come upstairs with a nightcap, his mind on his brother. "While you're in Galveston next week I thought it might be a good time for us to get this finally worked out about Harold." He settled himself on the chaise and took off shoes and socks; his tie was already on the bed. John always gets comfortable in my room. "Karl and Max said they could meet me down there, while the girls have their kids at the beach." The brothers share a beach house, where their wives and children congregate.

I was in a nightgown of rows and rows of Mexican cotton lace that looked like a christening dress, washed so many times it was as soft as a rag. Over by the window among the pots of ferns I was Rima in the forest, as my brother would say. From my green corner I offered to John what seemed to me an enormous revelation: "I may not go down for my birthday."

John did not register. His mind still on the preacher,

he said, "Well, sometime that weekend, then. We could drive down there together, and you could leave me at Harold's. No point taking two cars."

"I mean if I am going to stay home the brothers could come here." I stepped toward him with my hands sticking out from white cotton lace as though I was giving him a gift-wrapped present.

By this time John was down to his undershorts. He finished his gin on ice and frowned in the way that means he grasps I am trying to tell him something. "You're not going down there at all?" He had it.

"I thought I would have a party here. Wouldn't you like to have them all come, and Harold, too? I'm asking all my family." A decision I invented on the spot. Why not have them all.

"Well, sure." He looked delighted. "But that's a lot of work for you. You don't want to have to cook for all that crew."

"I don't mind; Nancy will help." I worked it out. "Mother and Daddy can stay at a motel, and Edward and Laura Ann can use the guest room, and, if they don't bring their families, your brothers can put up cots in Frank's room. He would like that."

"If that's what you want to do, that'd be great. They sure would like that. At Harold's we are always in the middle of some church thing." John did some knee bends, to get used to the idea. He put up his bar and chinned himself. Of his own accord he went down and brought me up some Cognac, in a dime-store orange juice glass with daisies on it. After a minute he reminded me, "That is Frank's weekend away, isn't it? I had figured that out if we drove down. You don't want him to miss everybody. Maybe he can switch around or something?"

"I'll call Franklin."

He did not like that. "Let the boy call; they can work it out."

I made him sit beside me; you can't have encounter with a gymnast. "John, I'm sorry that I made it worse downtown today."

He flushed. "It's okay. She said you brought her candy."

"That was my mistake."

"She'll get along; she's a bright girl."

"She cares a lot for you."

He looked guilty. "I guess I lead them on, without meaning to."

"John—I'm never going to be a Peggy."

"Well, I knew what you were like when I married you." He turned out the light.

Then, while the birdless sky lay dark and still and the risen moon held white and still, I laid my hair on his pillow and we made love gently, so as not to break the spell.

Afterwards, he said, "Do you remember the room we rented, from that old woman?"

"I remember."

"You remind me now of the way you used to look then, like you were happy and it didn't matter what a dump that room was, or how we were sneaking around. Like there wasn't any place else you wanted to be."

I hid my face against him, shamed that I was that content no longer.

"Mr. Hawkins, please." If Franklin's elderly secretary recognized me, she gave no sign.

"Franklin?"

"Hello, Ellen." He did, of course. "How are you?"

It was hard to hear his very familiar voice on the phone: the voice of a man I could have loved if I had known how. "I was wondering if you and Babs have any plans for this weekend." Nervous at calling, I had plunged into my request. "If you would like to take Frank now, instead of next weekend."

"Certainly, if you want him gone."

"No, I don't need—" He was making me into a mother who wanted her son out of the house. He bested me so quickly. "My parents are coming up for my birthday next Friday night, and I wanted him here to see them."

"Fine. Do you want to switch weekends, is that it? Or may we have him later on next weekend, too? We had not planned to drive up to the farm until Sunday anyway. Would your company be gone by then?"

"That would be all right. Why don't you work it out with Frank."

"Good, I'll give him a call." He waited, then added, "That's certainly a change, isn't it, for your family to come up here?" He was reminding me that he knew my habits well.

"Edward is coming down too." I didn't know what else to say.

"Have a good party, then." There was a pause in which he started to speak, but didn't. Finally he said, in a tone of dismissal, "Tell them hello for me."

"Thank you, and I'll tell Frank you'll check with him."

It was little enough as a gesture, one phone call. But it was the only way I knew to repay him for the cup of coffee. A looser arrangement with our son seemed a sort of handshake.

We were more civilized than I had imagined. It may be as Karol says: soon we'll have Franklin and his teacher by for drinks. Then Frank will have to deal with the new strain of all his adults being sociable; then the divorce will be truly final. Then we may not care at all.

As soon as I get back home with the sack of goods for Nancy, Karol appears to deliver her cheese ball and help us finish up the preparations. We move plants around, shift the heavy aspidistra, in an attempt to make a garden at one end of the sunporch, which will please my mother.

Karol says, "Seeing your ex- has suspended your judgment. You can't get all these people in one house. It'll implode and cave right in on your head. There's no way your Ed can make small talk with John's rube brothers. They won't have two words to say."

"It doesn't matter. The party is for John; he likes crowds."

"You should kill yourself for John Marshall?"

"I owe him a party."

"Men are good at that. They learn early to create the impression that you're not doing enough for them. Then when you do it all, they're off, leaving you like a discarded rind, to look for another peach."

"You sound a trifle peeled?"

No answer. She helps me arrange a jungle backdrop for the two extra tables with hemp cloths. Mother will see that the philodendron needs feeding. Her eye will scan them all and see the signs of my neglect. But it is too late now; no amount of plant food will restore them by suppertime. There is a limit to how well I can live up to her expectations.

Karol gets tired of greenery. It isn't her mother we are trying to please. We take a long break for coffee and talk about the hoard of relatives.

One foot out the screen door she says, "I hope it won't mess up your seating arrangement, but I've uninvited Nookie."

I count fingers. "That leaves thirteen."

"How unlucky, I've jinxed the Ball."

"I can move them around." I wasn't looking forward to Nookie oiling up Mother anyway. "Is this the end of him?"

She nods. "I know it's about time, but I move slow. It takes me a while to get there. I've spent three weeks building up in my mind how embarrassing it was the night with you all and Pete. Hell, I guess I knew before that: he's not the cream." She looks unhappy. "It's the same old story. I hang too many decorations on their branches. I have to build them up like J. C. Superstar and then I wonder why they can't support the weight. He's just a common salesman, is the truth."

"Didn't you ever know a salesman before?"

"Not socially. Not Biblically." She laughs, nervous at being unattached again.

"I'll seat you with Pete."

"I can't take him blowing his nose on Black Mama's seafoam cake. Find somebody else. How does your daddy like women in their prime?"

"Gravid. You can have your choice of brothers." Take them all.

"I hate young married men with babies."

"Harold is by himself, now."

"Can't you see me with a preacher? I'd have to start wearing homespun and my hair in a bun. If he wasn't so young, I'd go after Ed."

"Don't rule Harold out; preachers like invalid mothers."

"Which shows they don't have much sense."

My parents are the same as always. They diminish each other as they talk. One's parents' marriage is an argument for divorce. Nothing in the bending of their spirits to live out their lives for me through potting soil and the dinner plate made attractive to me a marriage that made less of me.

I kiss their cheeks for the adjustments they have made. They have stopped by on their way to freshen up at the motel.

"Who was that leaving out the back?" Nothing escapes Mother.

"Karol. You've met her."

"The loud one with the dyed hair?"

In the kitchen she nods to Nancy and accepts a cup of Sanka. "Wasn't that too bad about Edward?" she says, worried over her son, who has no issue.

"When I was up there I thought it was worse about Laura Ann."

Mother frowns. "You went to Dallas? I didn't
know." She does not like to be excluded from what her
children do. We are still supposed to check with her.
She observes the table in the dining room. "Sweet the
way you've done your setting. Who would have
thought to use all of mother's wine goblets as individual
vases. I must try that when I have sewing club. Don't
you think so, Daddy?" She includes my father, who is
eyeing the almond cake.

"Did you do the food?" she asks.

"Nancy's mother did the cake; she and I did the
rest."

"I remember that old woman, she made a delicious
cake for your wedding to John. I must have a little bite
tonight, and go off my diet." She intends to speak well
of Nancy's mother; making the woman who is not as
old as she by at least five years into a sort of catering
crone allows Mother to assume some charity for someone who is not only black but also as good a cook as she.

"Nancy remembered that you drank Sanka."

"Sweet girl." Mother smooths her flowered dress, a
summer linen with embroidered roses, and a matching
jacket that she keeps around her shoulders against the
air-conditioning. She looks around, frowning. "Hmm,
your philodendron looks a little under the weather.
You may need to feed it."

"Happy birthday, Ellen." Daddy gives me an absent
pat.

"I'm glad you could come, Daddy. No babies interfered?"

"I delivered a nine-pound boy an hour before we left." He is as proud as if it were his. "It was a breech presentation and the mother is doing just fine." He tries to make conversation. "Your mother was pleased to be asked up; John sure makes her feel welcome. But we're expecting you and the kids later in the summer." He looks to his wife, to have this verified.

"You will come down in July, won't you, dear?"

Frank comes in the door, stops short seeing his grandparents here ahead of time. Grayson, DeWitt, and Brewster trail right behind him. He handles all of us together clumsily, deciding not to try introductions, and escapes with his buddies to his room, after receiving a kiss from his grandmother, which he could not dodge.

Mother leans up to me and whispers, "Frank looks more like his father every day. I got quite a start when he came in the door." She looks down the hall. "Doesn't that bother John?"

"I don't think so."

"I should think it would; men have some pride about these things."

But we are not the ones to second-guess what men will value. I bend to kiss her powdered cheek for her concern.

. . .

The boys' bikes make the front porch look like a rental shop. From Frank's room their voices and their music carry. It is a rule I hadn't realized before: one boy is like a paramecium; he multiplies and then they multiply and then you have a pond full. I hear Frank say, "*John* told me that Uncle Fred got beat up by three guys at school. And that he put garbage . . ."

Loudly he has said John's name.

When his friends leave, the kitchen has four empty milk glasses, a trail of crumbs across the floor, and four fingerprints in the almond icing. On their way out there is a lot of door-banging and dust-tracking.

When we are alone, Frank, long-armed and bare-faced, stands around.

He trys to swing his arms like his Uncle Ed, or maybe he is limbering his shoulders like his stepfather. Whichever, he hasn't Franklin's way of standing still, of moving on decision. My son looks, in fact, most like an orangutan waiting for his supper.

"Yes?" Mothers get to the point.

"They're gone. The guys."

"So I see." I observe the floor.

"You want me to sweep or something?"

"That would be nice. You could dust off the bricks inside the door."

"Listen, were we supposed to get you a birthday present?"

"I don't think so. It's not that kind of birthday. You could look after Ellen Nor until they all come."

"I meant at the *store*."

"No."

"Dad said you said that I could go on back up to Nonnie's farm with them again on Sunday."

"Yes, I did." We have gone over this twice before. "You can go anytime, Frank. Anytime. I wanted you here to be a grandson tonight."

"Sure." He sweeps the dust around inside and then pushes it across the bricks with a dust mop that he shakes out when he is through behind the front hall table. This chore finished, he still hangs around. He follows me into the living room. It is apparent there is something on his mind.

"What, Frank?" I sit down, hoping that will calm us. My coffee has grown cold and tastes of mop dust.

"You must have liked *John* a lot." Again he gives a name to the man in our house. He gives it emphasis as he did to his friends, as though to be sure that we all hear him say it.

"I did. I do." I want to handle this right.

"I mean, you must have wanted to get *married* to him."

"I did."

175

He squirms on the slip-covered couch, throwing his legs over its arm. "I mean, did Dad just let you do it? Did he just let you go?"

These are such overwhelming questions. It is not the place for a mother's evasion: I must not be fake. I drink dusty caffeine, strain to do right. "Mostly, Franklin didn't want to move from you."

"He said when I get bigger I can go visit him in my car. He said I'd be getting a car in a few years." He has been promised a gift from his father.

"Yes. You can drive over whenever you like."

"John said it was okay, that Uncle Harold's kids were at his house more than at hers."

"You talked about this to John?" I can see that John made a story of it, making divorce at last a part of his own family.

Frank gets down on his back with the effort of our talk. He swings his legs over the couch back. "Well, he helped me when I got beat up. He helped me decide I might as well stay at my school as get it someplace else." He sits up, his voice unsteady. "If I was going to be gone a whole lot more I wanted him not to get mad about it."

"He wouldn't do that."

"Naw, he didn't. He said he felt bad about it anyway."

"He has from the beginning."

"I never thought about you all talking. I mean, talking about me and everything."

"Of course we did. We do."

He gets up, wrinkled from his ordeal. "Look, it's okay."

"Thank you, Frank." I stand too. Not as tall as he is. Not much more sure about things. It is awkward, not to hug or kiss. It is very difficult to let him know how much his blessing means. I touch his cheek and then drop my hand. "You could go see Franklin on your bike until you get that car."

"Clear across town?"

"Why not? At twelve."

He looks away. He is not able to deal with any more today.

I say to him, "Did you find the cookies in the kitchen? It will be a long time until supper."

"Yeah. We got hungry." He starts out, relieved to have it over. "That baby's going to sleep right through the party," he complains, back in character.

Frank has made it a birthday. Surely such an offering means another added year, whatever place one stands on at the time. Maybe when I am fifty he will put his arm around my shoulder and say, "Mother, here's what we bought you at the store." And his small daughters will fill my lap with gaudy, baubled necklaces, while their daddy, like John before him, tells some tale of other birthdays past.

From my room upstairs I hear a crowd of people gather as they always do when John comes up the walk.

When you get to a landmark on a trip it is proper to mark the occasion with a ceremony. An outward observance of an inner event. Two weeks after my party, in the greenness of our room, I have arranged a generosity on a silver tray. A silver bowl of roses, and crystal for our juice.

"In bed?" John pushes back the covers. He props his pillow behind him and receives, although he is more used to jumping up before me to do his knee bends on the rug. He is more used to moving and finds it hard to stay comfortable with a tray on his lap.

I pour us coffee in the English cups of veined old china that are saved for such times.

"Waffles? Pecan waffles?" He is delighted. "What's the celebration this time?"

But I don't want to spell it out. It is enough that I have prepared the uncustomary; let it stand uncommented on that we have got this far at least. We are crabs well past the second row of dunes. It is a long journey in human time: the clock says seven-fifteen.

"These are great," he says, "but you're not having any?"

One cannot change the given. I eat my wholewheat toast in the early morning sun as our allotted day opens blue and dry above the trees.

AFTERWORD

By James Ward Lee

In 1973, when Shelby Hearon published *The Second Dune,* she had been married for twenty years, which gave her a great deal of time to contemplate the life of an educated married woman living as adjunct to husband and children. An honors graduate of the University of Texas, Hearon spent a number of her married years outside the intellectual community she was educated for. She was a mother and wife, a Junior Leaguer, a member of PTA, a volunteer for Planned Parenthood, and a frustrated artist-in-waiting. Finally, in 1968, she published her first novel, *Armadillo in the Grass,* which set her off on a long and successful career as a writer. In that book, she began her exploration of the themes that mark not only *The Second Dune* but almost all the thirteen other novels that Hearon has published since. She is interested in the roles that women play and the disguises they wear to get through life, the relationships between husbands and wives, between mothers and their children, especially their daughters, and the often messy search for a "Prince of a Fellow"—to echo the title of her fifth novel. And always there are questions of appearance versus reality and free will versus determinism.

In _The Second Dune_, what we notice first is the relationship between Ellen, a somewhat frustrated housewife now on her second marriage, and her four-year-old daughter. The little girl, also named Ellen, wants a longer name, so she is always called Ellen Nor. Ellen Marshall hopes her child will grow up knowing that some of the things she herself was taught as a girl and young woman are false. She hopes Ellen Nor will avoid the traps she and many women learned from other women. She says,

> Raised by women, schooled by women, we who are mothers now were taught to look across the gulf to men and count ourselves only as they counted us. We learned to take our hearts and wrap them in ribboned boxes to be raffled at socials to the dark one on the right (p.6)

On the same page, she says, "Although we thus learned early to tune our ears to the language of men, it is from female to female that the Word is passed." But the problem is that too many mothers pass along the wrong Word, which says a young woman's only meaning in life is to be found in a relationship with a husband. In other words, a girl's job is to find a "prince" who will take her life in hand and lead her through marriage and motherhood and old age the way Ellen's father has led her mother. The way Ellen's brother Edward is dragging "his Laura Ann" from pregnancy and miscarriage to new pregnancies and more miscarriages. Edward needs to found a dynasty, and whether it kills his wife is of secondary concern. Less sinister but no less demeaning is the way John Marshall takes Ellen in hand and tries to re-shape her as the perfect suburban housewife. She had already been shaped once while married to Franklin Hawkins. But she kicked over those traces by having an affair with John Marshall and then leaving Franklin for John.

Ellen didn't learn her lesson the first time, but there are indications that she is now getting the point and will not stay forever with her second prince. Many things are changing in her life. In the past, she has always spent her birthday at her parents' house in Galveston, but this year she is not going back to the place where she relived her childhood and adolescence, wandering the dunes and swimming naked in the sea. Metaphorically, it seems, the first dune is her marriage to Franklin; the second is to John. She is living fitfully on the second dune but may be ready to return to the sea from whence she came, a sea where she had her own existence in some kind of geologic time. She says, quoting Einstein, that "time is not a constant thing. It depends on where you stand or whether you are moving toward it or away, a relative thing" (p. 4). And later on the next page—"time runs both ways at once, like the ocean's tide going out and coming in." We know—though Ellen may not have figured it out yet—that things have little chance of working out well between her and John. Their life is not *her* life. Ellen has her own ideas about life, and she is weary of adapting herself to the ways of men. Franklin was controlling in one way, John in another—even though she is not blameless in aiding and abetting them. Now, well along in life, she realizes that what she has learned from her mother's long marriage will not serve her well. Thinking of her parents' lives, she says, "My mother was not the best example of how to be a woman, as, through the years unable to get a response from my father, she mulched and pruned in compensation until she grew herself as dwarfed and mannered as a boxwood hedge." Ellen wants more, and she wants more for little Ellen Nor. What Ellen will ultimately do is not spelled out in the book, but it is pretty clear early in the novel that she is not willing to prune herself into a boxwood hedge or bear a vast family like the one John Marshall's mother provided to her prince. Will she, like the detested and soon to be ex-sister-in-law Velma, leave the Marshall clan? Velma leaves Harold, the preacher, for another man, and what is worse in the Marshall brothers' eyes is that she "didn't even leave his clothes clean or his dishes washed. And it was a Saturday night, the night before church, and he was working on his sermon" (p. 138). As she hears these complaints, Ellen thinks, "Not only adultery, but bad maid service. The mind grows faint."

In looking at the failure of marriages, Ellen has examples other than her own to contemplate. Most of the women in

the novel have succumbed to marriage or have run away
from it. She reflects on her mother, her sisters-in-law Laura
Ann and Velma, and her neighbor Karol, who is constantly
looking for a prince, but who is always finding a toad—her
last princely failure is a furniture salesman with the improb-
able nickname of Nookie. The women who serve as examples for Ellen are all victims of one female malady or another. The mother as a resigned boxwood hedge, Laura as a ter-
rorized mother-never-to-be, and Velma who fails as a maid
but succeeds as a runaway. And then Karol, on a pilgrimage
from bed to bed. Ellen is smarter than they are. She knows
she has to escape, but she won't do it with sex or submis-
sion. She has learned how both fail. So she must face the
prospect of striking out on her own. She tells us early in the
book about the annual pilgrimage to the sea: "I make an
annual trip to watch the world break whole, climbing a new
day over the edge of the sea, making me a year older. This
pilgrimage to home, to all of my earlier selves, has not varied through two husbands" (p.23). It is at the seashore that
"earlier Ellens lie, like surfaced fossils" (p.24). And, "There
at that water's edge are many Ellens" (27). It seems clear to
me that what we are watching in *The Second Dune* is the
shaping of a new and more mature and less dependent
Ellen.

Shelby Hearon is often reviewed as a novelist who writes
about mothers and daughters, but she is equally astute
about mothers and sons. In this novel and in others she

proves herself to be a close observer of boys and young men turning into the kind of prince who will steal some girl's heart and save her from spinsterhood or—worse still—genuine independence. Much of *The Second Dune* is spent looking at Ellen and Franklin's son Frank, who at the nadir of adolescence is struggling to find his bearings. As John, his stepfather, and Ellen's brother Edward sit and talk politics,

> Frank comes in to join us; he accepts a Sprite on ice, wanting to partake like the men in an after-dinner drink. I'm not sure who he imitates as he slouches down. It must be hard to try everyone's mannerisms on for size, searching for one that fits. It makes him seem so awkward, that not only is his voice changing, but his style is also, from room to room and audience to audience. It must take men a while to get comfortable with themselves: maybe they never do until they have a profession to put on for cover. (p. 52)

Here the question of disguises is applied to men and boys as well as to the women that Hearon puts in disguises so often. As Yeats says, we all must put on masks to conceal the real faces that we can't bear to have revealed to the world, or as Eliot says in his famous poem about Prufrock, you must "prepare a face to meet the faces that you meet." And since things are hardly ever what they seem, it is well to be prepared.

Men in Hearon's novels are never really savaged. They are as much victims of their culture as women are. Someone has trained them too. When Ellen visits John's office to take the box of chocolates to Peggy, the secretary who is leaving John's office because she has fallen in love with him, she muses that Peggy would have treated John better than she did.

> She made clear that a man like John—a Student Body President whose silver spurs still serve as bookends in his office—deserved better than he got at home.
> The fault was mine: I punished him for being what I most wanted. Married to Franklin, convinced that the confinement of our habits was imposed by him, not able to see that Franklin, accustomed to providing, must have constructed our routine to meet my needs, I had wanted John in my room. To inhabit it, to litter it, to undo my austere and scheduled existence. I had asked the Prince to ride up my glass mountain on his horse, and then withheld the golden oranges. . . .
> (pp.159-60)

Shelby Hearon does not provide easy answers. True, Ellen should not spend the rest of her life with John, but the fault lies more in the stars than in the smaller spheres of people. It is hard to say what she will do—and when. But things have a way of working out. Franklin, bereft at the loss of Ellen to John, has found Babs, who might be as perfect for him as Peggy might have been for John. And Harold, with the help of the Marshall brothers, may get over Velma, and maybe even Laura Ann will find the courage to escape Edward's tyranny. As Ellen says of Laura Ann's choosing her physician brother, "As was expected of her, she chose from all her suitors a tall, dark knight in a scrub suit. The trouble is that happily-ever-after is a country run by husbands, away from the footlights." But she also notes that "girls who know the right spells to cast can get out of their own towers without waiting for some passing prince" (p.81). And maybe they all will. But to wrap it up neatly is not Hearon's way. She makes the reader help her complete the book And that is what makes *The Second Dune* worth the reading.

William Halpern

About the Author

S helby Hearon was born in 1931 in Marion, Kentucky, lived for many years in Texas and New York, and now makes her home in Burlington, Vermont. She is the author of fifteen novels, including *Footprints, Life Estates,* and *Owning Jolene,* which won an American Academy of Arts and Letters Literature Award. She has received an Ingram Merrill grant as well as fellowships for fiction from the John Simon Guggenheim Foundation and the National Endowment for the Arts, and she has twice won the Texas Institute of Letters fiction award. She has served on the literature panels of both the Texas Commission on the Arts and the New York State Council on the Arts. Married to physiologist William Halpern, she is the mother of a grown daughter and son.